NIKKI TESLA AND THE
FERRET-PROOF DEATH RAY

JESS KEATING
ILLUSTRATED BY LISSY MARLIN

SCHOLASTIC PRESS

NEW YORK

Cataloging-in-Publication Data
Names: Keating, Jess, author.
Title: Nikki Tesla and the ferret-proof death ray / Jess Keating.
Description: New York: Scholastic Press, 2019. | Series: Elements of Genius ; 1 |
Summary: Nikki Tesla is a genius, so mostly she finds school boring, and
amuses herself by inventing things, like her mysterious missing father; trouble is
most of her inventions have serious, lethal potential (like the death ray, which just
blew a hole in her floor); so she and her ferret are hustled off to the special Genius
Academy with classmates who are equally exceptional, although she still worries
about fitting in—but when her death ray disappears she has something bigger to
worry about: who took it and what are they planning to do?
Identifiers: LCCN 2018035386 (print) | LCCN 2018037173 (ebook) |
ISBN 9781338295238 (Ebook) | ISBN 9781338295214 (hardcover)
Subjects: LCSH: Gifted persons—Juvenile fiction. | Private schools—Juvenile
fiction. | Inventions—Juvenile fiction. | Weapons—Juvenile fiction. | Fathers
and daughters—Juvenile fiction. | Secrecy—Juvenile fiction. | Detective and
mystery stories. | CYAC: Mystery and detective stories. | Genius—Fiction. |
Schools—Fiction. | Inventions—Fiction. | Weapons—Fiction. | Fathers and
daughters—Fiction. | Secrets—Fiction. | LCGFT: Detective and mystery fiction.
Classification: LCC PZ7.K22485 (ebook) | LCC PZ7.K22485 Ni 2019 (print) |
DDC 813.6 [Fic]—dc23

10 9 8 7 6 5 4 3 2 1   19 20 21 22 23
Printed in the U.S.A. at Berryville Graphics in Berryville, Virginia   37
First edition, July 2019
Book design by Keirsten Geise

This book is dedicated to you. Yes, you! The one reading this book right now. You're a genius, too, even if you don't realize it yet. Nikki and her friends are lucky to have you on their team.

That's me! I'll be drawing pictures for you! →

Leonardo da Vinci
The Polymath

Mary Shelley
The Writer

Grace O'Malley
The Leader

Albert "Bert" Einstein
The Visionary

Adam "Mo" Mozart
The Prodigy

Charlotte "Charlie" Darwin
The Biologist

Will Nikki Tesla, the Inventor, be their newest recruit? Read on to find out!

A NOTE FROM NIKKI TESLA

There's one thing you should know about being a genius: It can land you in deep trouble. We're talking in-over-your-head-poop-hitting-the-fan-you-better-hide-from-the-international-police trouble. Fugitive trouble. *Global meltdown trouble.*

You know what happens when you get in that kind of trouble? The government gets annoyed. They get their government-issued undies in a twist. They tell you that you must write a full account of said trouble for their records, *or else.* Because I'm not particularly interested in learning what "or else" means, I decided to listen. (You know, this time.) Luckily for them, I keep extremely detailed notes that will help me relive the whole story for them, like they were there for every hiccup, explosion, break-in. Every good scientist does. I can show you exactly how it happened.

So, I hope you're happy, government. Here's my story. I wrote the words. My friend, Leo da Vinci, is pretty good at drawing things, so he made the pictures. Let the official record show that I, Nikola Tesla, did not *intend* to destroy the world.

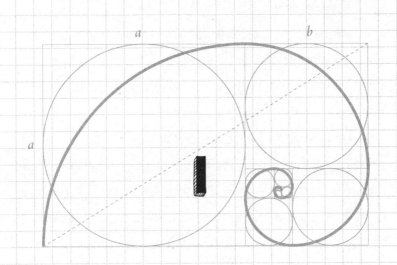

Okay, I can't really explain a lot right now because as you can see, there's a death ray pointed at my eye.

Yeah, a *death ray*. As in, utter destruction and annihilation—*poof,* you're dust!—all at the handy pull of a trigger on a weapon no bigger than a water gun. But this thing doesn't shoot water. Do me a favor and don't sneeze or anything, all right? I do not need to be vaporized right now.

In case you're wondering, the most important step when building a death ray is to keep your pet ferret away from it.

I learned this the hard way.

Pickles is my best friend. You might think it's weird that my best friend is a ferret, but I promise you she's very friendly and only bites when you startle her. Can you say that about *your* best friend?

She's escaped her cage twenty-seven times, so I'm pretty sure she's a genius. But she also eats her own poop sometimes, so maybe I'm completely wrong. Anyway, before I started working today I checked that Pickles was in her cage, and even filled it with French fries to make sure she would stay in there. But apparently the lure of

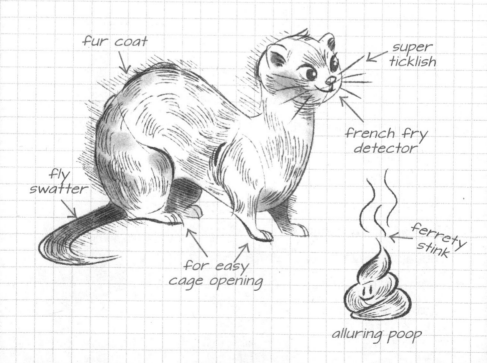

fur coat

super ticklish

french fry detector

fly swatter

for easy cage opening

ferrety stink

alluring poop

accidentally vaporizing me was too great for her. She jimmied the lock on the door and shimmied out of that cage with a mouthful of fries before I could say "Eureka!" Then that little so-and-so hopped onto my desk and started batting my death ray with her furry little paws.

The death ray slipped, and the next thing I knew, I was flat on my back with Pickles staring down at me, her brown paw resting on the trigger of the death ray like it was no big deal.

That brings us up to right now.

"Uh ... Pickles?" I squirmed against the floor, angling myself as best I could away from her aim. I was afraid to move too fast and spook her.

She cocked her head. Her tiny pink nose was snuffling. Maybe I should have given her gravy on those French fries.

"Would you mind moving away *slowly* from that gun, sunshine?" I asked her. I don't know why I bothered asking, really. She never listens.

"Come on," I coaxed. I glanced over to her cage. I was sure the pile of French fries was still inside, waiting for her. "Can't you smell how yummy those fries are? All greasy and salty. Triglyceride city. How about you go eat and let me clean up this mess? I'll even get you some gravy for them ...."

Pickles huffed. The trigger of the death ray clicked backward slightly as she adjusted her paw.

"Okay! Okay!" I winced. "Cheese, too! I'll get you some cheese, I promise!"

Pickles narrowed her beady eyes at me, and I started to wonder if holding me hostage for her cheddar fix had been her plan in the first place. She's had it out for me ever since I threw out the stinky toilet paper roll she used as a hat. Her ears perked at the sound of someone walking up the stairs.

Oh no.

"Nikki!" my mom yelled from the hallway.

"Don't come in, Mom!" I yelled back, my voice cracking traitorously. Pickles and my mom didn't get along very well. The last thing I needed was for Pickles to get panicky. Not with the barrel of the death ray still aimed at my eyeball. Plus I'd *sort of* promised my mom that I wouldn't mess around with any new inventions anymore ever. Especially dangerous ones.

I was pretty sure a *death ray* wouldn't be seen as a safe gadget to her, no matter what cool stuff it could do.

My doorknob twisted. One surefire way to guarantee your mom comes into your room is to tell her to stay out.

"Don't come in?!" Mom burst in, already in full rant

mode. "Young lady, as long as you're living under this roof—"

Her mouth dropped open when she saw me on the floor. Above me, Pickles gnawed on the trigger of the ray gun. This was some bad luck right here. I really should have put a safety on the thing.

"Mom!" I hissed. "Don't *move!*"

But it was too late.

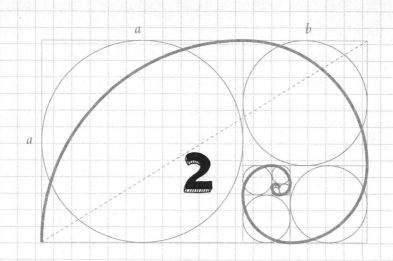

I blinked up at my ceiling, digging my fingernails into my blue rug. Particles of soot and dust swirled and danced in the air. The smell of burnt wood and plastic stuck in my nostrils.

Nostrils!

I could smell! I'd made it out alive!

You were worried for a second there, weren't you? I mean, *I* was. The minute Mom came storming in, I thought I was going to end up like extra-crispy fried chicken.

But I was okay. I couldn't say the same for my bedroom floor, which now had a three-foot hole in it, opening up into the kitchen and living room below. The explosion also shattered my bedroom window, leaving jagged glass and bits of wood frame scattered on the floor.

Whoops.

"You've always said you wished our house had a more open layout." I tried to joke with Mom to lighten the mood. I wish someone would invent Mood Lightener for situations like this.

I had managed to roll away from the blast before Pickles could do any bodily damage, so my mom should have been *happy*, right?

But the look on her face told me otherwise.

"Nikola. Angelina. Tesla." She used her scary voice. The one that makes the hair on the back of my neck stand on end.

This wasn't good.

"Yes, Mom?" I knew where this was going. It wasn't the first time I was going to get The Lecture.

I tried to look extra innocent. It's not easy when the tip of your hair is on fire. I swatted it with my hand until it stopped smoking.

"What have I told you about your science experiments?" she said. Pickles began to nibble on the hem of her pant leg, but Mom was too angry at me to notice. This was also not good.

"No dangerous inventions," I recited. "No incidents. No accidents of any kind. Stay off the radar."

"And what does that *mean*?" she continued.

I took a deep breath. "It means nothing that can injure, maim, disfigure, dismember, impair, cut, scrape, bruise, blast, blow up, or vaporize anyone."

"Or . . ." She glared at me. If it were physically possible for steam to come out of her ears, I was pretty sure she'd be steaming.

"Or anything that can set fire to our house."

"And what part of that did you *not* understand?" She

used the toe of her shoe to stamp out a tiny fizzle of spark on the floor.

I shrugged. My mom knew as well as I did that *not understanding* something wasn't the problem.

I'd been tested a bazillion times by all sorts of people in white lab coats. I'd answered surveys, done written tests, and even had interviews with all sorts of kid psychologists. The answer to what was wrong with me? I understood *everything*. One hundred percent comprehension. That's why I got bored in class so often. And that's why I liked to spend my time making cool inventions. Can you blame me? Tell me that you wouldn't make a death ray if *you* could.

Mom rubbed her temples with her fingertips. "Nikki, I didn't argue when you wanted to use the Wi-Fi modem to make some wireless invisibility machine. Or my hair dryer to develop some . . . some—"

"Telepathic car starter," I finished for her, pursing my lips. I'd been so close with that one. Imagine being able to start your car with a single thought! Much cooler than a silly hair dryer. *Air* dries hair; why do we need a special machine?

She frowned. "But this is getting to be too much. Just last week you promised me you'd stop this dangerous

stuff after you nearly destroyed the oven. You're going to blow the house up!"

"Technically, the ray wouldn't blow it up. It would vaporize it. Like the hole in the floor here." I tapped it with my foot. "Those atoms are toast."

"What do you even *need* something like this for?!" She reached for the ray gun. "What *is* this?"

"Don't touch it!" My fingers clamped on her arm. "It's a death ray. I don't *need* it for anything."

Mom's eyes widened. "A *death* ray?!" Worry lined her face, and instantly my mouth went dry. I knew what she was thinking.

"It's n-not like that," I stammered in a panic. "That's just a name for it. Sounds way worse than it is, I swear. It's a glorified Nerf gun."

She blinked at me, clearly not buying it. "Why would you invent such a thing?"

"I didn't invent it for the *death* part, Mom! It's the technology! If I can figure out the best way to concentrate the particles, then it's one step closer to free energy for *everyone*! Can you imagine?! Everyone on the planet! Think of the possibilities for—"

Mom cut in. "But a death ray, Nikki?!" she continued. "Do you *really* need to make one of these?"

"Do we *really* need microwaves? Or planes?" I blurted. I knew exactly what Mom was worried about, but the technology behind the death ray was what I cared about, not the stupid thing itself. Didn't we have a responsibility to see what was possible if it could ultimately help humankind? Mom sure didn't see it like that.

"I promise—it wouldn't have blown a hole in the floor if Pickles hadn't knocked it over and pinned me to the ground with it."

Pickles, the traitor. I should revoke her French fry privileges.

"But the neighbors," she said, peeking outside my window. She lifted the charred, wispy curtain with her fingertip and immediately let it fall again. "They're already starting to . . ."

My cheeks began to burn. I hadn't thought of that. Of course the sound of the explosion and breaking windows would catch their attention. I looked outside and cringed at the sight. A handful of nosy neighbors were beginning to congregate in the fronts of their yards, like a fidgety flock of hungry seagulls. Some girls my age, a few adults—their cell phones aimed high at our house, no doubt eager to film the gray smoke that was beginning to escape. I swallowed down my guilt and turned away from the window.

"We've barely just moved in, Nikki. All it takes is one viral video and the news crews will show up . . ." She ran both of her hands through her hair and held them there for a moment, her eyes closing. I knew what she was picturing. The flashing camera lights. The microphones shoved in our faces. The photographers camping out behind the fence.

"Four houses in three years," she whispered. "It's hard enough keeping our privacy without these incidents."

She didn't need to remind me. The anxious, noisy chatter of our neighbors drifted up at us, nipping at my worry like an obnoxious dog.

"The newspeople won't show up," I said, clearing my throat. "It was just an accident, and nobody knows about last time. *Or* who we are," I added. "I'll fix the floor, I promise."

The sound of the doorbell made us both jump.

I shifted on my feet to get a peek through the hole in the floor. "Are you expecting someone?"

Mom crossed her arms over her chest. "No," she said, lifting her chin ever so slightly.

A tiny worm of suspicion wriggled inside my stomach. My mom wasn't one to lie, but whenever she did, she lifted her chin like that. I first figured that out when she told me my goldfish, Susan B. Anchovy, had mysteriously up and left on a *vacation*, rather than going belly-up in her tank. I also knew that weird little chin lift because it was exactly the same thing *I* did when I lied.

Mom avoided my eyes. "I'll go do some damage control with the neighbors," she said, tiptoeing around the singed floorboards.

The usual guilt coursed through me as I saw the disappointed look in her eyes. Nothing made me want to crawl into a hole like that look. "Tell them I slipped in the shower?" I offered weakly.

She pursed her lips and turned on her heel. "Clean this up," she ordered. "And be careful. The last thing we need is you hurting yourself by falling through the floor."

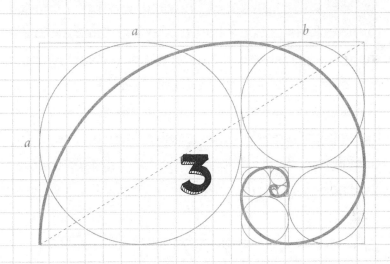

She was almost right. Falling through the hole in the floor would have been bad. But what was *actually* the last thing we needed?

The man with the fuzzy microphone aimed directly at Mom's face when she opened the door.

"Mrs. Tesla! Mrs. Tesla! Your neighbors called in about a noise complaint. Can you comment on whether that was an explosion?" The man's voice echoed through the house.

"Nooooo!" I spat, diving to the floor. Pickles, thrilled with the thought of having me on her level, scampered over my back and began stuffing a French fry in my ear.

"Get off!" I whispered, shoving her away. I crawled to the hole and did my best to stay quiet and avoid the shards of glass, sweeping them out of the way with the arm of my shirt. If I craned my neck and kept as low as possible, I could just catch sight of the guy. He wore a red-and-black jacket with a news logo on the chest. Behind him, the black lens of a camera peeked over his shoulder.

total jerk!

"Vultures," I muttered to Pickles. "How did they get here so quickly?!"

Mom wasn't having any of it. "I have no comment whatsoever, and I'll thank you to get off my property before I alert the authorities." Her voice was as sharp as the glass on my floor.

Yeah! Go, Mom!

She pressed the door to close it, but the man stuck his foot out, jamming the door open. "What a *jerk*," I said, my lip curling in disgust. I crawled over to the window again. Sure enough, a white news van was now parked in front of our driveway. More than a dozen neighbors milled around, pretending to do various things to their lawns while they spied. *Nosy vultures.*

Then, the question that sent a chill down my spine.

"Mrs. Tesla, given her previous issues, are you worried that your daughter is following in your husband's footsteps?"

My jaw dropped, and even Pickles seemed to halt when she heard those words. I flattened to the floor again and listened with every cell of my body. I didn't need to see Mom's face to know she was beyond done with this guy already.

"What's your name?" she said sweetly.

"Rick Roeper, with WKGM News," he said, holding his microphone closer to her face.

"Uh-huh," she said, edging closer. Her voice was dangerously low. "Well, Rick. This is the second time I'm asking you to get off my property before I call the police."

She shifted her weight to kick his foot out of the door-frame. "And it's *Ms*. Tesla. And that's *ex*-husband."

She slammed the door shut, and I used the noise as a cover to haul myself up from the floor. Pacing with Pickles on my shoulder, I cursed myself for being so careless. Why hadn't I listened to her? Why couldn't I just lie low like she'd asked me to do a hundred times before?

I already knew the truth, but that didn't make it easy to face it. When I wasn't working in my lab, I felt like a rat in a maze with no end. Like I was suffocating. What was the point of science if we couldn't push the limits?

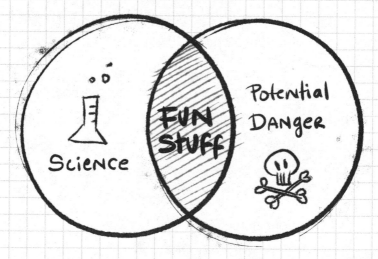

Another knock at the door sent my panic soaring again.

"Go away," I urged the reporter, peeking again outside. The white van peeled away, leaving the neighbors looking disappointed. They began to head back inside their homes. A black car with dark windows now sat parked in the driveway. Police?

I held my breath, waiting for the telltale signs of cops at the door.

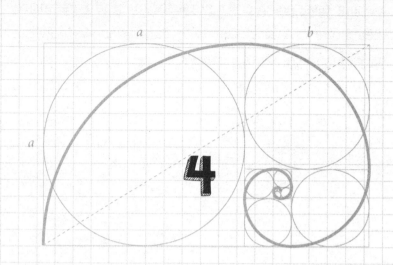

Good news. It wasn't the police at the door.

Bad news. It was so much worse.

Have you ever seen those movies about the men that protect the world from aliens? They show up at houses in their black suits and sunglasses looking all mysterious? When I snuck a peek downstairs, that's exactly what I saw. Two men in dark suits. Serious resting snitch face. Mom must have sensed they meant business, because she let them in and showed them into the living room to sit awkwardly on our sofa. They had small earbuds in their ears, connected to wires that ran into the collars of their jackets.

My stomach began to rumble, and it wasn't from hunger. Fear began to drain away, leaving intrigue in its place.

Was the president here to visit me? Had she heard about my inventions? Maybe she wanted to hire me as her resident weapons designer and protect humanity.

I knelt closer to the floor so I could listen. Mom had poured two glasses of iced tea for them, which sat untouched on our coffee table. If she was offering beverages, they definitely weren't reporters.

"Ms. Tesla." The larger guy spoke first. "It's come to our attention that your daughter has been creating some . . . weaponry . . . that could pose a threat to the community, or worse. We're here to discuss her options."

Pickles nattered quietly in my ear as I struggled to eavesdrop. Options? What did that mean?

Ooh. Maybe they could give me a better lab space.

"You may as well come join us, Nikki." Mom raised her voice to call me out. "It's your future we're discussing here; you shouldn't be eavesdropping about it."

Shoot.

I grabbed Pickles and hoisted her farther onto my shoulder and checked my hair quickly in the mirror on my wall. I looked like I'd lost a fight with a chimney, but once I'd wiped the sooty marks from my face, I thought I could pass for a kid who had been playing outside in the dirt rather than one who was up to no good with potentially fatal weapons.

I kept my head high as I marched down the stairs.

"Oh, do we have visitors?" I asked. Look at me, all innocence and light.

The big guy didn't seem to buy my act. "Ms. Nikki Tesla, I presume." He flipped open a black notepad and jotted down something quick and scribbly. I was dying to squint and lean forward to see what he'd written, but didn't want to risk looking too nervous. Grown-ups can smell fear. Especially ones in suits.

ear bud
so super-
secret
spy leader
can talk
to them

fear
detector

spy
camera
in tie

"Do you have any idea why we're here?" the second man asked me. He hadn't removed his sunglasses in the house, so I couldn't look him in the eye.

"You're selling Girl Scout cookies?" I crossed my arms over my chest.

They exchanged a glance with Mom. One of those "can you believe this kid?" looks. I didn't much appreciate it.

"Nikki..." Mom warned. "Be nice."

Dude #1 started to talk. "We're here because we've been watching you, Ms. Tesla."

I squirmed. This was almost as scary as having Pickles's paw on the trigger of my death ray again. What did that mean, *watching me*?

"Okay," I said. I fought to keep my face neutral.

"We know about your inventions. The car starter, the telescope that can see through walls." There was a pause. "And the death ray."

I gulped, shifting on my toes. I had the right to remain silent, and I was darn well going to use it.

"We're here to offer you the opportunity of a lifetime: admission into a specialized school that can provide the resources you need to be successful in life."

I considered this for about 2.4 seconds. "No thanks," I said. "Not interested."

"Nikki, you should listen," Mom said. Her face was pulled into a tight grimace. Usually when people showed up to snoop around our house or my inventions, she got rid of them pretty quick, just like with that reporter guy. But this time she bit her nails, eyeing the two men nervously. My stomach started to flip-flop.

"We think you might want to hear all the details first," the man continued, pointing to the chair. "Have a seat. Now."

It wasn't a request.

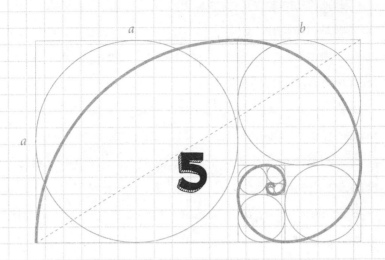

I perched awkwardly on the arm of our big blue armchair. Even Pickles was quiet, curled up like a furry scarf around my neck. I was beginning to wish I'd trained her to bite on command. Maybe a Rottweiler would be a better laboratory companion.

"All right," I said. "I'm sitting."

The smaller guy kept talking. Well, I say "smaller," but he was still approximately the size of a fridge, very tall with wide, bulky shoulders that threatened to burst out of his tailored suit. "We believe that the academy would be a wonderful opportunity for you, where you could use your gifts for the betterment of society." His voice carried the mellow lilt of a southern drawl.

"The academy?" I scoffed. "What, like a private school or something?" I reached up to Pickles automatically, searching for her scruffy fur. Nothing made my stomach twist in knots like the word *school.* "How do you know I'm not bettering society right here in my own house, huh?" I peeked up at the hole in the ceiling behind them. The smell of burnt floorboards was still wafting through the air.

"I'd hardly say that blowing up your home is for the good of society, Nikki," he said.

"Vaporizing," I mumbled. I squared my shoulders. "Sorry, guys." I scanned their jackets for signs of holsters or guns. They were each wearing one by their left armpit, and it looked like another was strapped to the insides of their right ankles. Good to know. "I'd rather stay here. Thanks." I added the last word as a courtesy to Mom. And because of the guns.

Okay, mainly the guns.

Both men frowned, and Dude #1 shook his head. "It would also be a place where you could interact with peers."

I blinked at him, my stomach winding tighter. "Peers? Meaning *kids*?"

He nodded. "Talented, intelligent kids, Nikki. I'm sure you'd quickly become friends with them."

Friends.

I squeezed my hands into fists, digging my nails into my palms. Clearly these two suits didn't understand the first thing about me. About why I was even home-schooled in the first place. The last time I was in a school with kids? Please. Do you know how kids treat anyone who's smarter than them? I'd spent more time shoved into lockers than I cared to admit. Those things are *not* hygienic, by the way. Gum everywhere. Also a bizarre rotten-fish smell. Where the heck does that smell *come* from?

"I don't really . . . *get along* with other kids," I said, shoving the horrible memories from my mind and avoiding Mom's eyes. "I never have, and it's kind of something we need to accept. Sorry."

Mom's head bowed, and for a moment, there was no sound in the room. A flush of shame crept over me, but I held my chin high. That tiny movement made a small piece of the puzzle click together in my head. The look on her face when she'd heard the doorbell. I turned to look at Mom.

"This is no random visit, is it?" I asked. Sweat began to prickle on my palms.

Mom held my gaze for a millisecond, then cracked. Like I said, she'd always sucked at lying. "Nikki, *please*," she said, her shoulders drooping with defeat. "I think you should listen to these men! This could be an amazing opportunity for you!"

"*You* called them!" I shrieked. "You want them to haul me off to some— some *academy* for nerds so I'm not your problem anymore? Is that it?! Because of the stupid floor?"

"Nikola! Of course not! They got in touch with me months ago, and I told them I wasn't interested! But lately . . ." Mom stood up and rushed over to me, gripping my shoulders. I jerked myself away, backing closer to the kitchen. My throat was getting dangerously tight, and I knew when that happened, tears weren't far behind.

"I want you to be *safe*, Nikki!" she said. She pointed to the two men, who sat watching us, calm as two cucumbers in suits. "You deserve to be in an environment where you can learn all you like, about *everything* you want, so you can chase your dreams! The academy could give you that! And above all, it could be a safe place for you to be yourself, among other kids with gifts like your own!"

My lip curled in disgust. "Kids. Gifts. Right." I licked my parched lips and shook my head. She had no idea what she was asking. "You *want* to send me away to a boarding school. Just like that. All because I accidentally messed up our floor—"

"It's not the floor!" Mom's fist came down on her hip. Her cheeks shone red and her lip trembled. Immediately, her face softened. "It's *you*. And me. And how best to help you. I love you more than the world and want you to be anything you dream of being—but, Nikki, I need you to be *safe* while you do it! I don't have the resources here to help you! Our house and, more importantly, your well-being can only survive so much!"

"Is this because of my father?" The words popped out of my mouth before I could stop them. The thing everyone was thinking. The horrible truth. My dad, the so-called brilliant professor who'd died when he accidentally blew up his entire laboratory. They'd discovered his remains there, along with a notebook describing his plan to detonate the bomb in the city center.

Awful, right? Not only had his own invention destroyed him, but he wanted to use it to hurt people. I could barely remember him, but I still have the vivid image of Mom collapsing into a heap after hearing his name on cable news one night, with the notebook the police had found. Ever since then, we'd been running. Trying to get away from his name, his memory, and his awful legacy. That was seven years ago, and to this day, every time I picked up a beaker or welding torch, I knew she worried I had the same madness in me.

I knew I didn't, but that didn't stop others from assuming the worst of me.

"I heard that reporter, you know. Everyone thinks I'm turning into him, and you want to send me away because of it!" I snapped at her.

Mom's face fell, and my heart began to crush in on itself. "This is *not* about your father," she said softly. "You are *nothing* like that. I just want you to have the opportunities you need to succeed."

I gawked at her for a moment, then the fact that we weren't alone seeped back over me. I refused to cry with those stupid strangers in the house.

"I need something to drink," I croaked, stepping backward. Any excuse for an escape. I made it all the way to the kitchen cupboard, leaving them behind in the living room, before I noticed that I'd stopped breathing. Mom's muffled sobs drifted around me like a bad dream that wouldn't disappear after waking. I reached into the cupboard and found a glass. Gripping it in my hand, I glared at my fingertips as they turned white against it. It would take nothing to break it—just like that it could shatter.

"No, it's okay." One of the men was consoling my mom, his voice barely a whisper. I turned on the faucet, letting the cold water overflow the glass onto my fingers.

"I'll go talk to her," Mom said. There was a creak on the floor as she stood from the sofa, but her footsteps halted before the kitchen.

"No, ma'am," one of the men said. The one with drawly voice. "Allow me. Please. Maybe go outside with Mac and get some air? Just for a few minutes. Why don't you give Nikki and me some breathing room in here?" Then there was the sound of more shuffling, and the front door screen swinging open.

I took a huge gulp of water and forced my features into an unshakable mask. I could sense the big guy's presence behind me before I even turned around.

"I'm not changing my mind," I said to the air. I crossed my arms over my chest and turned to face him. His sunglasses were still perched on his face.

"You're going to want to hear what I have to say before you decide that," he said.

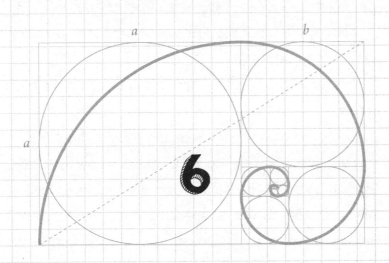

6

For a guy in a fancy suit, he didn't pull any punches.

"Look," he said, his southern drawl thick. "I'm not s'posed to tell you any of this, y'hear? So keep your mouth shut for a minute so I can get this out before they come back inside." He twisted around to check the front door. The shadows of Mom and the other guy shifted beyond the glass.

"First of all, yes, your mom did call us. And you know what? She's perfectly justified in wanting help for you. It ain't easy having a genius as a kid. Two, we know all about your inventions, Nikki. I know you've nearly perfected the ray. We've been following you for a long time, and *everyone* here is in agreement that Genius Academy is the best choice for your future."

I snorted. "Not *everyone*. Don't I get a vote?"

He cocked his head. "Everyone who isn't a minor, then," he replied.

I resisted the urge to stick my tongue out at him. Barely.

"How did you even find out about me?" I asked.

He cocked an eyebrow. "Come on, now," he said. "Brilliant kids with dads like yours don't go unnoticed in this corner of the world, 'specially when they're paired with inventions that can blow up a city block. You might have your ma's name, but that kind of history is pretty easy to track down."

"Dad," I muttered. "Figures. That's not why I invent stuff, you know?" I said, desperate to defend myself. Not *everyone* who was smart used it for evil reasons.

"Now, I know that," he said, patting me on the shoulder. I shrugged away, staring angrily at my glass of water. "But you gotta admit, it looks bad, Nikki."

"Only to people who aren't paying attention," I seethed.

"Listen," he continued. His voice dropped low. "There's more you don't know. Now, I think you're a pretty smart kid. You got your father's smarts—that's clear by the hole in the floor, ain't it? So I'm going to tell you this and trust that you're mature enough to handle it, okay? No freaking out or telling your mom or crying about it."

I narrowed my eyes. "I'm smart enough to know I shouldn't be talking to strangers," I said. I knew I was pushing it, but I couldn't help it—trapped in a kitchen next to a Lurch wannabe in sunglasses wasn't high on my list of fun ways to spend an afternoon.

"Nikki, be *serious*," he hissed. "There are consequences for your actions today." He darted another look at the door. "You've drawn too much attention with these stunts. Too much media, too many prying eyes. It ain't right, especially given who your father is."

I glared at him.

"*Was*," he corrected. "If you refuse our offer and don't go to the academy, the government reserves the right to confiscate any and all materials and products that you've invented. This includes your notebooks, any documents of your research, and computer files."

I practically choked on my tongue. "You can't take my stuff! I worked hard on those inventions! You can't steal someone's research!" Instantly, my mind's eye swept through my room—hundreds of hours of work scratched in my notebooks, just sitting up there for anyone to take. I edged slightly back out toward the living room, ready to protect my lab.

He tilted his head down at me and lowered his sunglasses just a smidge, revealing a pair of bright blue eyes. "Actually, we can. And I wasn't done. If you do not join us, your mother will also be imprisoned for a period of no less than five years, for aiding the manufacture of dangerous unregulated weaponry."

"*WHAT?!*" My breath caught in my chest as I sputtered like an idiot. "You can't do that! None of this is *her* fault. It was all me. That's not fair!" I started to storm out to find her, but the man's arm reached across the doorframe, blocking me in the kitchen.

"I'm afraid it's true," he said. There was a note of embarrassment behind his eyes, but also eagerness. "I wanted you to have all the information. This isn't just about your future, kid. It's about your mom's, too. The government takes unregulated weaponry of this caliber very seriously. She could face serious jail time." His arm dropped from the doorframe, but I was rooted to the spot. "Don't you see? I'm trying to *help* you, kid."

Guilt stormed through me like an army. All these years Mom had tried to protect me from people getting nosy about my life and my inventions, especially after Dad died. Going through all those homeschool tutors.

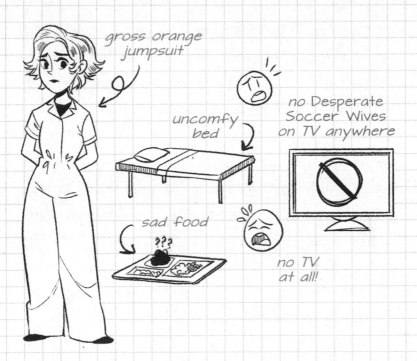

gross orange jumpsuit

uncomfy bed

no Desperate Soccer Wives on TV anywhere

sad food

no TV at all!

All those moves from town to town. And now I could be the reason she went to jail?!

Tears began to pool in my eyes, but I wiped them away angrily. "I can't go to this school." Angry flashes of gossipy, nasty kids began parading in my head.

"Nikki, with your skills and knowledge—your inventions—you could be a wonderful addition to the academy. You would be welcomed and your gifts would be encouraged," he said.

I didn't reply. I was too angry. Too defeated. What good was making awesome inventions if they landed you in so much trouble?

"Wouldn't it be nice to feel *challenged* for once at a school that can help you?" he continued. "To not be so bored that you spend all your time rereading the latest X-Men comics in the back row like you did in second grade?"

"How do you know about that?"

"Ms. Tesla, we know everything about you." His voice softened a notch. "Please come with us. You won't regret it. You'll be joining other children with . . . gifts like your own."

"Gifts like almost blowing up the house," I said.

He cracked a small smile. "Precisely."

The sound of the front door opening startled me. Standing taller, I struggled to find a way through this predicament that wouldn't end with my mom in jail *or* me at some lame school for nerds. But one look at Mom's face and my resolve crumbled.

"I can't let that happen to her," I whispered. I mean, I didn't like her silly "don't invent weapons" rules, but all in all she was a great mom. I let her down so often, but she still stuck by me and tried to do her best. Now it was my turn to repay her, I guess.

The man ushered me back into the living room to meet them. "Remember," he whispered in my ear. "You and I did not have this conversation."

"Have things calmed down a little in here?" the other man asked, looking more than desperate. Mom came over to give me a big hug.

"Yes," I said, forcing myself to keep a stony face.

The suit I'd been speaking to nodded at me. "Nikki and I had a nice chat about the wonderful kids she'd get to meet, if she chooses to attend the academy. All attendees must go of their own free will," he said. "We have no choice here. But you do. What do you think, Nikki?"

My shoulders slumped. It was decided, then. He'd given me a gift—letting me know the real consequences of saying no. I wasn't about to squander it.

"When do I need to leave?" I asked.

Mom's face flushed with relief, but there was a clear sadness behind her hug. "Oh, sweetie, I'm so happy that you're willing to try this." Tears began to well in her eyes. I bit my lip to keep from joining her. The man with the sunglasses gave me the tiniest smile of satisfaction. He looked relieved.

The other man looked at his watch. "We'll send transport in one week's time," he said. "You can bring anything you like, including all your lab materials, as well as any pets." He edged away from Pickles, who was batting one of his shoelaces with wild abandon.

my awesome
shield

no shield

You'd think that I would feel a huge wave of relief. I wasn't getting arrested today, and neither was my mom! But the truth was, I'd rather be going to jail than to school with a bunch of judgmental, prying, cliquey twelve-year-olds. I closed my eyes for a moment, envisioning a weapons-grade shield growing around me to protect me from whatever was to come.

My shield hadn't let me down in years, but this would be a massive test. Death rays were one thing, but other kids? Nothing was scarier than kids.

"And what's this place called again?" I asked.

"Genius Academy, Ms. Tesla. You're going to love it."

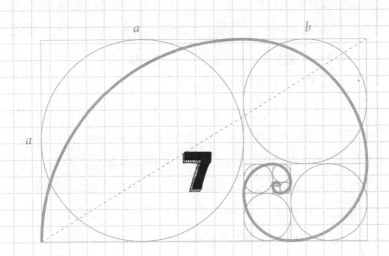

I dropped my suitcase next to Pickles's travel cage on the marble floor of my room and gawked at what would become my new home. So far, it was pretty swanky.

Genius Academy is an eight-floor limestone mansion located on sprawling green grounds in ███████████.

Did the censors black that out? I bet they did. See, technically, I'm not allowed to say, or even *write*, where Genius Academy is. It's some government rule, so I bet by the time this story gets to you, there are missing bits. They even covered my eyes when they brought me here, but I managed to figure it out by counting the hours and modes of transportation from home (two cars, one helicopter), and comparing that against the species of trees lining the grounds. I'm not allowed to tell you that Genius Academy has ▇ rooms, ▇ bathrooms, ▇ laboratories, ▇ helicopter pads, ▇ swimming pools, and even an ice cream truck.

Oh. I guess I *can* tell you about the ice cream truck. It's one of the few perks I'm happy about, because according to the sign, they serve my favorite, Rocky Road.

But as for what I'm actually supposed to *do* here at Genius Academy, I'm not too sure. The only thing they've given me so far is this fancy room. There was also a small scroll on my bed, with a list of classes I'm supposed to attend. It was so long, it rolled down to the floor when I untied the little blue bow that held it together.

"What the heck?" I read the scroll. "Is this some sort of joke?"

I was talking to myself, but a woman's voice cut in behind me.

"It's definitely not a joke, Ms. Tesla."

"Geez!" I whirled around, practically leaping out of my shoes. "Don't do that! Creeping up on me like some ghost."

The woman held her hands up in apology and stepped inside the room. She was very tall, with close-cropped silver hair that stood out against her dark skin, and wrinkles around her mouth and eyes. She wore a blue

INTRODUCTION TO WORLD LANGUAGES

ADVANCED LOCK PICKING

CODING YOUR WAY OUT OF TROUBLE

ART HISTORY

GENETICS, GENOMICS,
GEOGRAPHY & GERANIUMS

MUSIC APPRECIATION

ENGINEERING FOR DUMMIES
(JUST KIDDING. IT'S FOR GENIUSES)

LEADERSHIP & MANIPULATION

ADVANCED QUANTUM PHYSICS

ASTROBIOLOGY

THE WRITTEN WORD & YOU

TRAVEL TIPS FOR THE BUDGET-
CONSCIOUS EXPLORER

COUNTERINTELLIGENCE...

pantsuit, the same shade as the bow on the scroll, and spotless black leather shoes. Her clothes immediately made her look immaculate, but it was the look on her face that told me she was in charge around here.

She stood stick straight, and extended a hand out to me.

"Ms. ▮▮▮▮," she said. "But you can call me Martha." She smiled warmly.

I reached out to shake her hand. "I'm Nikki," I said. "And you can call me Nikki." I wasn't trying to be a smart aleck. Okay, maybe a little bit. I was still peeved about the whole "threatening to lock up my mother" thing, after all. But this woman looked like she could dropkick me to China, so I kept my snark in check. How the heck did she sneak up on me like that, anyway?

She dropped my hand and took in my new room. "I trust that the accommodations are to your liking? There is a full-service cook on the fourth floor for all your dining needs. Breakfast is at seven thirty, lunch at noon, and dinner at seven every night. Classes take place on the other levels at various times throughout the day, all of which I'm sure you'll enjoy once you get into the swing of things here. In the closet, you'll also find appropriate facilities for your . . . ferret, is it?" She eyed Pickles, who was just waking up from a snooze. "Do you have any questions before you begin?"

Do I have any questions? Hah. Yeah, how about, why on earth am I in some top secret government mansion, huh? Let's start with that.

I knelt down and released the latch on Pickles's cage, letting her climb up to my shoulder. I expected someone as straightlaced as Martha to be put off by the sight of her, but Martha surprised me by reaching out to scratch Pickles under her chin. Of course, Pickles reacted appropriately, baring her teeth and hissing.

Just kidding. Pickles loves attention, even if it comes from the matron of my imprisonment. She happily lapped up those scratches like a spoiled house cat.

"How many students go here?" I asked. The most important question: How many people was I up against?

"Six. You will be our lucky number seven."

I blinked at her. "Seven? That's it?" Doubt began to unfurl inside me. The grounds and school were huge. How on earth were there only seven kids here? I couldn't decide if I should be excited, because six kids to deal with was way better than a giant schoolful, or upset, because six kids likely meant they'd be super cliquey, which was even *harder* to handle.

"Seven, including you. Yes. That's *if* you fit in here. Which I'm sure you will." There was more than a hint of warning in her voice, which made me stand up a little taller. "If you take a look at your desk and in your closet, you'll find plenty of tools to help you succeed here, as well as your complete wardrobe from home. Academy students

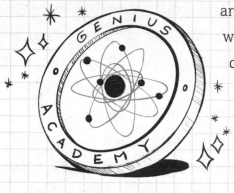

are permitted to wear whatever clothing they desire, but we do ask that you wear one of our academy accessories every day." She adjusted a small blue pin on her lapel. An atom with six electrons circling the nucleus. Carbon.

"Is that one of the academy accessories?" I pointed to the pin.

"It is." She smiled. "In our experience, simple accessories like these help our students feel like they're part of a team, but there are other benefits to a good accessory. Here, allow me."

She removed the pin carefully and affixed it to the collar of my shirt, giving Pickles another quick pet. "Lovely. Consider it a gift."

"Thanks," I said. I twirled the pin with my fingertips. To be honest, on the list of things that really mattered to me, accessorizing was somewhere between reality television and the color of my shoes. Accessories didn't *do* anything, so what was the point? I decided to keep my opinion to myself.

I followed her over to the desk in the room, a spotless flecked-marble surface that reflected the sunlight from the window. Gold knobs adorned the set of drawers on the left side, and a small lamp hung down from the ceiling over the space, creating a soft yellow glow. The whole room belonged in a magazine about fancy-pants workspaces. It made my bedroom at home look like a crime scene. My hand lingered on the desktop. If the rooms were this beautiful at Genius Academy, how amazing were the lab spaces?

"Open the top drawer," Martha said. Her eyes twinkled.

I hesitantly touched the handle of the drawer. If I was too eager to check the place out, she would think I was happy to be here, which I wasn't. But curiosity got the best of me. I pulled the drawer open and peeked inside. Pickles hopped down to investigate, too.

"Laptop, notebooks, schedules, a state-of-the-art research database connected to the other students, as well as top professionals in all fields of science and humanities around the world," she said. "You'll find everything you need here to succeed. Of course, after your orientation, you'll get to see your private lab space."

My eyes widened. "I . . . I get a whole lab to myself?" My thoughts exploded into confetti. Accessories were pointless, but my own *laboratory*? That was life changing. Images of all the inventions I could develop bubbled up in my head like a fizzy drink, giving me something much more thrilling than a sugar high. *Think of what I could create.*

"Is that what I'm supposed to do here, then?" I tingled with excitement, but fought to keep my face straight.

"Among other things, yes," she said. "Everyone is expected to take part in school activities as required."

"Everyone," I repeated. "Right." Every other kid here had a room just like mine, and probably a lab space of their own, too. A dark thought crept in before I could stop it. "The rest of them," I said. "The students, I mean. Do they know, um . . ." I drifted off, biting my lip.

Martha tilted her head. "Do they know what, Ms. Tesla?"

I forced my chin higher. "Do they know about my . . . history?"

Her face softened. "Your father."

I nodded, grateful I didn't have to spell it out any further.

The corners of her mouth barely tipped up. "No, Ms. Tesla. You share your mother's maiden name, and we firmly believe that each student makes their own destiny here, regardless of where they came from. Your history, as well as the media coverage of your father, is safe. You may share your secrets with those you choose."

I breathed a sigh of relief. "Okay," I said. "Great."

I would be choosing to share my secrets with no one, thanks.

Her eyebrows knit with concern. "You should know that your fellow students will not judge you, Nikki. They've all had difficult moments in their lives, often because of their intelligence and inability to blend in with, shall we say, *normal* society."

I shook my head, eager to change the subject. "I get

it," I said. I didn't want to mention that it didn't matter what they were like—I wasn't here to make friends.

She clapped her hands together suddenly. "Oh! I almost forgot. Laundry." Her shoes clacked on the floor as she stepped around behind my bedroom door.

Laundry. My shoulders sank. Not nearly as thrilling as lab space.

"This is your laundry bag," she continued. "*Every* student is in charge of their own washing, is that clear? Machines are on the fifth floor." She clicked her tongue. "We're happy to tend to your minds here at Genius Academy, but we believe that good habits like laundry are also very important to our young globe-trotters."

"Globe-trotters?" I stared at her.

She shook her head and reached out to grab my shoulders, giving them a light shake. "Oh, don't worry about that now, Ms. Tesla. We're so happy to have you here with us. But you'd better get a move on! Orientation testing begins in ten minutes!"

I blinked at her. "Huh? I forgot there was going to be an orientation. All I got was that." I pointed to the scroll on my bed. "And a *pin.*"

"That's because every orientation is specifically designed with the new student in mind! Failure during orientation results in immediate expulsion. You don't want that, do you?" she said in a singsongy voice. Her personality turned on a dime, going from friendly and open to no-nonsense and firm. "Now, scoot!"

She was talking about my mom going to jail, but there wasn't a trace of anger or irritation on her face. I couldn't risk it, so I did the only thing I could think to do: I bolted out into the hallway and began searching for my orientation test. Pickles leaped from the desk to scurry after me.

"You need to go to the pool on the sixth floor!" Martha's voice carried through the marble hallway like a stern bell.

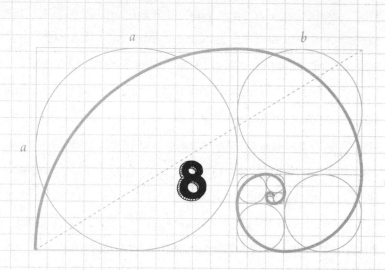

My heart was slamming in my chest when I finally made it up to the sixth floor. The smell of chlorine hung thickly in the air, clawing at my throat and nose and making me pant. That, or racing up three flights of stairs, showed how totally out of shape I was.

Let's go with the chlorine.

I skidded to a stop outside a huge set of white doors, nearly crashing into a man who paced wordlessly back and forth. He wore a blue jacket like Martha's, and a pair of loose-fitting track pants. Instead of shoes, he wore rubber flip-flops. Another atom pin was stuck on the collar of his raggedy white T-shirt.

"Nikki!" he said. "I'm Geoffrey. That's Geoffrey with a 'Gee-off.'" He gripped my hand and shook it once. "Glad you made it! We've been waiting for you. Oh, is that your ferret, then? Hello." He bowed ceremoniously to Pickles, who was slipping and sliding on the marble floors like they were made of ice. "You might want to be careful on these polished floors, Ms. Pickles."

Geoffrey yanked open the door and nudged me inside toward the pool.

Did I say pool? I meant POOOOOOL. The thing was *huge*! You know those swimming pools that Olympians use? This pool was even bigger, flanked with a whole wall of floor-to-ceiling windows that let sunlight stream in. A warm breeze that must have been pumped in gave the whole place a tropical feel. Suddenly my future was filled with inflatable pool donuts and umbrella drinks.

Maybe this Genius Academy thing wasn't so bad.

"Whoa," I breathed. "This is amazing."

Geoffrey clapped his hands together. "So glad you think so. Right this way. We'll get your orientation started immediately. I recommend your ferret chill out on the lounger while you're occupied."

His flip-flops slapped against the tiled floor as he power walked toward the far side of the pool.

"Wait," I said, rushing after him. I tugged my shirt away from my skin as I shuffled across the tile, already sweating in the humidity. "I don't have a swimsuit or anything. What exactly will I be doing for orientation?" Images of me standing half-naked in my underwear by the pool had already started to pop up in my mind. What kind of orientation takes place at a pool, anyway? I wasn't trying out for a swim team here.

"Tut-tut," he said, wagging his finger at me over his shoulder. "No spoilers!"

That's when I noticed the cage.

It was about ten feet wide with totally transparent walls, and was suspended on a metal platform above the water. The weirdest part? It was filled with *kids*. Six kids to be exact, all wearing the same Genius Academy blue, but in totally different ways. One girl had a blue bandana wrapped around her head. The three boys wore blue shorts (cargo, board, and basketball, respectively) with matching blue wristbands, and another girl had on blue overalls, with a polka-dot tank top underneath them. One girl even had blue streaks in her hair. That seemed to be taking the academy dress code a little far, if you asked me.

All six of them looked like they didn't belong anywhere with *Genius* in the name. In fact, they looked like the world's geekiest sports team. But even worse was what they were all doing. They were *waving* at me.

Ummm.

"What's with the cage?" I asked. My feet had a mind of their own, and I slowed down to a trudging pace. Did I mention that I have claustrophobia? Yeah. That might explain why my pulse was racing like a cheetah as I gawked at that thing. Who's got two thumbs and wasn't getting into a cage suspended over water?

This girl.

"Reinforced plastic!" Geoffrey said proudly. "For your orientation! Come! Come!" He reached the cage and knocked on the side of it with one hand and yanked me closer to the small set of steps with the other.

I eyeballed the kids inside. They were all waving and smiling through the transparent walls, and their voices rose above the open top. "Hi, Nikki! Come on in!"

I stepped back.

Yeaaah, no.

I didn't need to be a genius to know the chances of me getting inside that waterlogged death trap with a bunch of weirdoes were zero. And how did they already know my name? The idea that they'd been told about me ahead of time made me feel even more unprepared. It wasn't fair that they knew who I was but I had zero idea who they were. I mean, they were smiling and not being mean to me at all, but if they were okay with being stuck in a cage suspended over water like this, there was one thing I knew for certain: They were completely bonkers.

"Don't be afraid. You only need to hop in for a quick minute!" Geoffrey said. He started to hoist me up the ladder by the elbow.

"Wait!" I yelped. "I just have to go in for a minute, right? Because of my claustrophobia? I've got to prove I can handle it. Is that it?" My armpits started to prickle with sweat. My deodorant was working overtime already. I tried to calm my breathing, but time seemed to be racing forward without me.

"Something like that!" Geoffrey said. He leaned into my ear to whisper. "*0-1-2-1-1-9-0-3*. Now, *up* you go! Remember: Any student who fails orientation is immediately expelled!"

"Huh? What?" I yelped.

He had said it with a smile, but that didn't stop the dread from growing in my chest as something clicked inside me. *Expelled.* Meaning Mom goes to jail. My head was spinning too much from the thought of the tiny cage to think straight. I took a huge breath and tried to picture Mom's face. The last time I was in a tight space was the ball pit at McDonald's when I was six, and that was only because I wanted to calculate how many balls were in there, *not* because spending time leaping around in a pit full of boogery plastic balls was my idea of fun. Toddlers are disgusting, you know. Full of phlegm and influenza viruses.

Okay. Focus.

Keeping my eyes locked on my feet, I let Geoffrey boost me up onto the small step so I could swing my leg over the top of the box. I hopped down in the middle of the group of kids, lamely clutching my arms around my chest. *Do it for Mom*, I repeated in my head. *Do this for Mom.*

"Uh, hi," I said. What else do you say in this situation? *Nice cage you got here?* This day was getting crazier by the second. *Keep breathing, Tesla*, I reminded myself. The edges of my vision were getting a little too swimmy and blurry for my liking.

"Are you nervous?" the blonde girl in the blue overalls asked. There was a spray of freckles across her nose, and her British accent caught me by surprise. With her squeaky voice and darting eyes, she reminded me instantly of a mouse. She also wore an atom pin, but hers was pinned to the strap of her overalls. "You look really scared. It's okay, we don't bite."

I tried to smile, but I'm sure it came out like a twisted grimace. How long had it been since I'd been around people my own age? Two years? Three? This group didn't know that I was planning on sticking to myself once classes started up, just like I had in regular school.

The tall, lanky boy cackled. "My research indicates that nearly one hundred percent of people are hesitant to enter into unfamiliar circumstances in front of an audience, Charlie," he said. "Particularly when bodily harm is imminent or likely."

I gawked at him. *Imminent or likely?* Neither of those described any type of bodily harm I was comfortable with.

Tucking my arms close to my sides, I wished more than anything that I could have done my orientation alone. It was awkward enough being at a new school without this "meet everyone" nonsense. I seriously had to get working on a teleporter one of these days.

"I don't like small spaces," I admitted. "So I think this orientation is a test to see if I can handle this box." I took another deep breath, and looked down below our feet. There were small waves lapping in the pool, but as long as I kept breathing slowly, I could keep my nerves in check. It would all be over soon.

"You think so?" The girl with spirals of blue-streaked hair and dark skin poked her head around someone's shoulder. She had the hardened, logical look of someone who had been in her share of tight spots, without a trace of fear on her face. "Usually our orientations are a bit more intense than that. They're designed to test out how you react in stressful situations and how well you work with others—"

She didn't have time to finish.

A low groan sounded above us.

"Hey!" I said. "What's he doing?!"

Using a pulley above our heads, Geoffrey hoisted a single transparent plastic sheet over us. On its side, it almost look like a—

I gasped. Geoffrey maneuvered the hard plastic sheet on top of the box—the *lid* to our box—and began bolting it on.

Bolting! As in, with *bolts*. Totally secure and impossible to remove from the inside. We were locked in like trapped rats.

"Wait!" I said. I scrambled to the side and pounded on the plastic. "Let me out of here! Nobody said anything about a *lid*! Stop! *Gee-off!*" I jumped as high as I could, but my fingertips couldn't reach the top to haul myself up. "Hey!" I shouted and pointed at the tallest kid. "Jump up there and stop him!"

"Don't be afraid." The brunette in the bandana squeezed my arm. She yawned, like she was lazily feeding ducks at the park instead of stuck inside this box. "There are air holes everywhere." She pointed to the tiny pinprick holes surrounding us. "Plus you can see everything outside!"

Somehow Little Miss Mellow wasn't making me feel any better. "How long do we need to stay in here?" Sweat poured down my back, collecting in the waistband of my jeans. "This isn't exactly a normal orientation, you know?" I tried to laugh, but it came out as a nervous bark. The walls, despite being perfectly transparent, seemed to be closing in on me. I closed my eyes, forcing myself to breathe deeply.

"That's for sure," said a sandy-haired boy behind me, making me jump again. "For Grace's, they dropped us in the middle of a storm on a dinghy in the Atlantic Ocean!"

The kids all nodded happily at the memory.

"What?!" I gaped at the group. "You could have died!"

They shrugged, and the boy continued. "Genius Academy isn't exactly a normal school, in case you haven't noticed."

Something stopped me from rolling my eyes at his easy expression. Something *loud* and lurchy. My center of gravity was going haywire. I didn't need to look down at the water to know what was coming next.

"Oh, you've got to be kidding me," I wailed. I didn't care how scared I sounded. I was about four milliseconds away from peeing my pants. The platform holding our cage up above the water began to tip. We were hovering over the water dangerously, edging off the platform.

"Everybody ready?" the blue-haired girl called out.

"Ready for what?" I panicked, holding myself upright by pressing hard against the wall of the box. "No!"

"We're going in!"

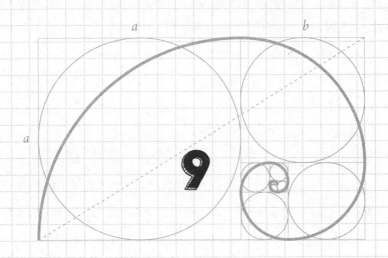

9

"Into the water?!" I squeaked. "But the box is bolted shut! There are air holes! Do the math, guys—we're going to drown!"

"Uh-huh!" the sandy-haired boy said, stretching his neck like he was preparing for a big race. "It's fun!"

Fun.

My blood turned to ice. These people were bananas. Somehow, my mother and I had been totally conned. This was all one big scam. There was no other explanation. Maybe I was on a television prank show, where they put people in horrible situations just to watch them freak out. I squinted through the plastic, looking for hidden cameras.

"Yeah, okay," I said. I'd heard enough. I pounded the side again. "Excuse me? Geoffrey! Gee-offrey or whatever! I'd like out of here right now, please! Or I'm . . . I'm *calling the cops*!!" Geoffrey was nowhere to be seen, so I resorted to something pretty desperate. "Pickles!" I shouted. "Pickles, go get help!"

The girl with the blue-streaked hair patted me on the shoulder. "Just go with it," she said. "It's a lot easier if we work together, I promise. It's totally natural to be scared."

"And who exactly are you?" I spat. "Someone who doesn't value her life, clearly." I darted a look at the water below us. The platform was moving at a snail's pace, but we were definitely getting closer and closer to the water.

She looked me square in the eyes. "Orientation changes all the time, but it's always hard," she said. She stuck out her hand. "I'm Grace. Grace O'Malley. Guys!" She raised her voice and clapped her hands. Everyone in the box quieted down almost instantly. The only sound was the water below us, rushing closer by the second.

"Everyone say hi to Nikki before we take our plunge!" she instructed.

"No!" I said, jumping to claw at the top of the box again. "I don't *care* who you all are. I care about getting out of this thing! There will be no *plunging*!" My voice had the shrill edge of a girl about to totally lose it.

"Oh, come on," Grace said. "Everyone say hi!"

At her command, a chorus of greetings rang out. Our cage groaned as everyone jostled to get a better look at me and say hello.

"Hi, Nikki!" the sandy-haired boy said, reaching over to pat me on the shoulder. "I'm Leo!"

"And I'm Charlotte Darwin!" the English girl to my left squeaked. "But you can call me Charlie."

"I'm Mary Shelley. Happy to meet you!" another voice called out. I think it was the girl with the bandana. "And that big guy to your left is Mo!" she continued. I jerked around, eyeballing a boy who'd been silent this whole time. He was muscly and wide, with dark eyes and short hair. He smiled feebly at me, but didn't say a word.

Good thing, because I wouldn't have had time to answer, anyway.

The platform holding us tilted on its side with a lurch. "Here we go!" Grace yelled.

It took only seconds for our cage to tip into the pool, sending a massive *whoosh* of water across the surface. The lights in the ceiling went all swirly as the box groaned and heaved. Tiny rivulets of beaded water began to stream into the cage and down the sides, collecting at our feet. A whole orchestra of emotions surged through me. Anger that I'd ended up in this stupid position. Annoyance that everyone was all smiles and greetings despite how dire the situation was. And absolute terror that this was going to be the end for me, stuck in a plastic cage with strangers who all somehow knew my name already.

"Not good!" I squeaked, scratching the side of the plastic wall in vain.

We were sinking.

And soon, we would be drowning.

Tell my mother I love her!

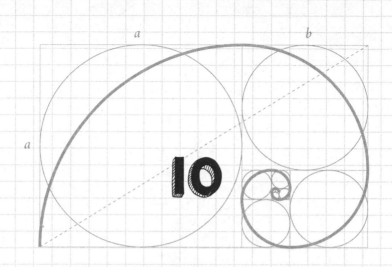

The box bobbed in the water for a few harrowing seconds before dipping deeper. There was enough air inside to keep us suspended, but I squeezed my eyes shut anyway, trying to calculate how long we had. Judging by the amount of water on the floor already, it was less than six minutes.

"This isn't funny anymore, you guys!" I said. I hopped on my tiptoes and tried to bang the top of the box. "Help! Can anyone hear me?!" Pickles, ever the loyal companion, launched herself off the lounger and into the pool. But, ever the completely *useless* companion, she was just doggy-paddling around, clearly enjoying the quick dip.

"Wow," I muttered, realizing the unfolding truth. "I'm going to die in this box and my ferret is going to watch it happen."

"All right," Grace said. "If we don't find a way out, we're toast. Where do we go from here? Tesla, did Geoffrey give you any clues?"

I couldn't believe what I was hearing. We were about to go the way of the *Titanic* and she was thinking about clues?

"This isn't some Sherlock Holmes mystery," I snapped. "This is a sinking box! We're going to *drown* down here. Start smashing the sides at hard as you can! There's got to be some way we can apply force in the right way!" My brain was scrambling for a way out, but the surprised looks on everyone's faces distracted me. In case you're wondering, it's impossible to think straight when you're about to die. Just for the record. Pickles continued to paddle around us, unaware of my imminent demise.

Mary frowned. "The whole point of this is to work together," she said. "Yelling and freaking out won't do us any good."

The rest of them stared at me like I was trying to solve a math problem with a Popsicle instead of a calculator. They were totally confused. And worse than that, they all had sad smiles on their faces. Were they feeling *sorry* for me?

"It's true," the lanky guy said. "Many hands make light work. Most peer-reviewed studies support this." He wagged his bony finger at me.

"Are there any peer-reviewed studies about breathing underwater? Because we're going to need to in a minute!" I yelled, pounding the side of the box. Water had begun to pool around my knees. "Maybe you guys don't have a good reason to get out of here, but I do not want to die this way. I have a mother! And . . . and a *ferret*!"

"We usually get some kind of clue for these tests." The tall boy stuck out his hand. "I'm Bert, by the way. Did Geoffrey mention anything to you earlier? He often says something odd that sparks an idea for us. If you can tell us that, we can start thinking on it. We'll have a much greater chance of success if you can provide that information." He shifted on his feet, clearly unfazed by the rising water level lapping at his pockets.

I rolled my eyes. "Don't you think I'd remember if he'd told me how to get out of this thing? Now, can we start shoving, *please*?"

Nobody moved. The water was up to our waists now, and the bottom hems of our shirts were starting to float lazily on the surface of the water. I was officially going crazy. My mom's face popped into my head. I wondered what she'd make of this whole mess. Her kid drowning to save her from jail. It sounded like a soap opera. A *bad* one.

"All right," Grace said. "If that's all we have, we'll go through wall by wall." She turned to me. "Fair enough? Start on the front wall. Everyone look for any imperfection you can find. Weird seams or marks. Anything."

It was enough for me. Now that Grace was on board, the group followed suit. In an instant, everyone navigated to the right and began examining the edges of the wall with their hands. If I wasn't terrified of meeting my watery doom, I would have marveled at how quickly she got everyone on the same task.

"There's got to be something we're missing here," I grumbled to myself as I held my breath, diving below the waterline to inspect the bottom of the box. It was hard to see without goggles, but I didn't notice anything weird about the seams.

I started to panic, accidently swallowed a mouthful of pool water, and began to sputter. The guy named Leo caught my elbow and yanked me above the surface. The water was up to our shoulders now. At this rate, I calculated there was an 88 percent chance I would die within the next two and a half minutes. But I couldn't let myself give in to panic. I *couldn't*.

I forced myself to think straight. I was a genius at Genius Academy—whatever that meant—so I *must* be smart enough to find a way out of here. I couldn't count on these strangers to help me. What had I missed? Had Geoffrey given me any hints?

I hacked on another mouthful of water as the other kids kept searching for a way out. They were getting frantic now, kicking to stay above the waterline. Worry began to leak onto their faces faster than the water around us.

"Nikki!" Mary said. "Are you *sure* that Geoffrey didn't say anything to you? We're getting to the eleventh hour here!"

"I'm thinking!" I squeezed my eyes shut. I ran through everything I'd seen or said between arriving at the pool and hopping in the box. As water lapped at my chin and gravity released its grip on me, I tried to laser my focus. Then, finally, *lightbulb.*

Eleventh hour.

A number. That's what Geoffrey had whispered in my ears. My brain raced to conjure it again. Eight digits . . .

01211903.

It didn't make a lot of sense, even to a genius like me. But at least now I had something to go on.

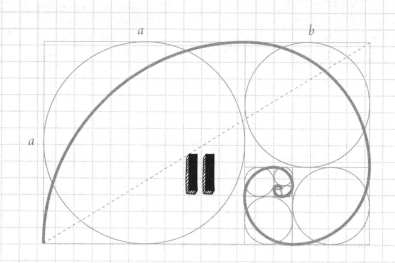

"Wait!" I yelled. "He gave me a number! It's 0-1-2-1-1-9-0-3!"

"Got it!" Grace nodded once and barked an order. "Bert! Mo! Do those numbers mean anything to you?"

"Could be a code," Mo said, struggling to stay afloat. Charlie was clinging to his shoulder, kicking hard to keep her head above water.

"There isn't a keypad to input a code in any of these walls." Bert shook his head, sending a trail of water through the air. "Could be a sequence of letters. A equals 1, B equals 2—" he began.

"That's no good," Mary interrupted. "There's no letter to denote zero!"

"Does it relate to a book?" Grace asked. "Maybe it's the Dewey decimal number!"

Mary coughed a mouthful of water, shaking her head. "Nope," she said. "The number's too long. Maybe it's a weight or unit of measurement? Something we could use to leverage the sides open?"

I racked my brain, which I was learning wasn't an easy task when you're half-occupied with treading water. 0-1-2-1-1-9-0-3. Clustering the numbers together in different ways, I tried to chase down the pattern. 012-119-03. 0121-1903. 01-21-1903.

Wait. That was *it*.

Beside me, Leo seemed to arrive at the same idea. "It's a *date*!" we said in unison.

I beamed at him. "January 21—1903! It's gotta be Houdini, right? That famous photo of him all chained up was taken then."

He narrowed his eyes in concentration. "His most popular escapes were in water. This has to be—"

"The plate glass escape! *Yes!*" I yelped. A thrill zipped through me. I wiped water from my eyes with one hand. The mottled lights on the ceiling swirled above us. My breath came only in quick gasps. "Check the hinges! The hinges on the back wall. If we're right, there should be hollow bolts that we can unscrew, and we should be able to push out of here!"

Now that we had a solid plan, everyone jumped into action. But I wasn't going to relax until I was out of this cage and back on dry land. My hands moved fast. The rising water was above my chin, sending chlorine fumes up my nose.

"Everyone!" Grace yelled out. "Deep breath on three—two—*one!*"

I sucked in a humungous breath with milliseconds left. Our cage was completely submerged, full of water. Everything went silent. Without gravity tugging us down, everyone was swimming and trying not to knock into one another as we checked every bolt and hinge. My heart began pounding faster than it ever had, like it knew I was on my last few seconds of oxygen.

Mary grabbed my shoulder from behind, and tugged me to her corner. Pointing to her hinge, she gave me a thumbs-up. She had it!

I couldn't say anything underwater, but I didn't have to. The whole team was tuned in, part of the same electrical network sending messages back and forth at lightning speed. Within seconds, Leo and Bert were unscrewing the false bolts, while Grace, Charlotte, Mary, and I pushed against the back wall with the last of our strength. Finally, the muscly guy, Mo, gave one shove with his shoulder.

The hinges broke free. The back wall sank to the bottom of the pool in slow motion, landing flat on its side. Bubbles caught in the seams trickled up to the surface. I'd never been so relieved in all my life, but my chest was about to explode without air.

Clawing the water, I followed the trail of bubbles and took off for the surface as fast as I could, bursting out of the water like a sputtering sea lion. Behind me, the others rose all at once, locking elbows and clinging to one another. They were coughing and breathing hard, but everyone was still upright.

I hauled myself out of the pool, collapsed onto the cold tile, and sprawled on my back. Tiny red and white stars popped in my vision.

"That," I sputtered, "was *nuts*." I tried to let my heart calm down. "What is wrong with this place?!"

Grace climbed out of the water using the ladder and helped everyone else out before answering me. Her springy blue streaks were dripping trails of water onto her shoulders. "I know it seems weird, Nikki." She lifted the bottom of her shirt to wipe her face. "But it's really important for us to be able to work together as a team here. You did a good job with that Houdini clue—you just need to learn to share things with us and trust us to help you! Orientation is all about getting to know every-one. Using one of your biggest fears is a good way to do that quickly."

The others all shook their heads in agreement. "Yeah," said Leo. "You have to admit, you won't forget our names now!"

Please. Like I'd been paying attention to any of their names. "And why is it so important that we work together, huh?" I threw my arms up. Droplets of water flung from my fingertips to the glass windows beside us. The reality of what had just happened was crashing over me. I scooped up a sopping wet Pickles from the pool and wound her across my shoulder, wishing I could have an actual shield against people instead of some crummy, imaginary one in my head.

"I've been in school before—I didn't care about anyone's name then and I sure as heck don't intend to start here!"

The clacking sound of high heels on tile interrupted my rant. Martha marched toward us, carefully navigating around the puddles of water that we'd splashed across the floor. For a second, I wanted to yell at her. This was her fault, after all. But then I saw the look on her face, and my cheeks got hot.

She was *not* happy. In fact, she was scowling.

"I'm sorry to interrupt." Her voice was soft, but her eyes were narrowed into thin slits as she looked directly at me. "Please find some dry clothes and make your way to the Situation Room. I'll meet you there in twenty minutes."

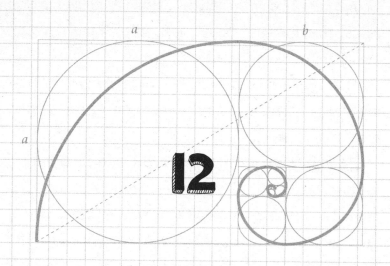

I was out of one hot mess and into another.

Martha was going to expel me. I was sure of it. Wasn't that what Geoffrey had said? Failure at orientation meant you got expelled. It was obvious they wanted this place to be all about teamwork—even Grace had said that—and then I had to go and mouth off to everyone. It had to be obvious to Martha that I wasn't fitting in. She was probably watching from some perch above us all, waiting to see if I messed up my initiation. Why had I been so stupid? I should have tried harder to connect with the others.

The only thing left to do was make my escape. I tried the window in my room, but it was locked tight. I had no choice but to meet my fate. After changing my clothes, I made my way to the Situation Room on the top floor.

The other kids were standing together in a group, waiting for me before going inside. Grace was the only one who looked me in the eye. So they were mad at me, too.

"Before we go in there, what's the Situation Room?" I asked, resigned. I was stalling for time. I didn't want to face my mother after this. Nearly drowning was one thing, but getting expelled and sentencing her to jail time was even worse.

"It's where we deal with . . . situations," Leo said.

I frowned. "I'm pretty sure that I'm the situation here. Let's get this over with."

Grace pulled open the giant door and led everyone inside. The long room was all marble, like the rest of the academy, but at the end of it was a single desk. Martha's desk. Seven chairs sat in front of it in a big crescent. Computer screens and digital maps lined the walls. In the middle of it all, Martha leaned on the edge of the desk, her expression unreadable.

The way she avoided my eyes made me flash back to the last time I'd been in school. It was years ago. But the image of my teacher's embarrassed face was seared into my memory, along with the shame and guilt that racked

me as I tracked in behind my mom, my fingers still covered in tiny smears of mustard from my sandwich at lunch.

Third grade.

Ms. Kirkpatrick.

She hadn't been embarrassed because anything had happened to her. She'd been embarrassed for *me*. As I'd picked away at my yellowed fingernails and stared at my feet, Ms. Kirkpatrick unloaded the truth on my mom. Mom, the one who was voted "Most Popular Girl" in her school. They didn't think I could make out what they were saying from where I sat in the hallway, but I can still remember every word.

Hushed whispers. Sad sighs. Nikki eats lunch alone in the bathroom every day. Nikki doesn't fit in well with her peers. Despite our best attempts, Nikki has a hard time making friends. Nikki is very smart, but she is a target for bullies because of it.

The boiled-down version of all that?

Nikki doesn't fit in here.

As it turned out, "here" didn't only mean that school. It meant *every* school, and soon, it became clear to Mom that homeschooling and private tutors were the only way to help me learn without the hassle of other kids bullying me, especially when news about my dad started making the rounds. Four schools in three years all said the same thing.

You would think the worst part about it was the bullying, right? Being picked on, used in school for test answers and then ratted out as a cheat, or finding your latest projects in the toilet of the girls' bathroom.

But that stuff wasn't even close.

The worst part was the forced smile on Mom's face as she walked out of Ms. Kirkpatrick's classroom. "No big deal," she'd said, shrugging. "The programs here aren't up to snuff, my little smarty-pants. We're going to find you some *fun* teachers to visit at home from now on."

She tried to make it sound like her idea, but I knew the truth. She was disappointed I couldn't make friends.

Disappointed I wasn't like her. Because isn't that what all parents want? For their kid to be like them? She was a popular kid all through school, yet somehow she'd been given a colossal loser as a kid. I couldn't blame her. I'd be disappointed, too. If I ever knew what it felt like to fit in, I mean.

That was the day I decided to build a shield. Something I could bring with me, everywhere I went, like I was a warrior or a knight. I imagined it to be made of the most powerful, indestructible substance on earth, capable of protecting me from anyone or anything that wanted to get close and hurt me. It might seem like a cliché, but it was the only way the equation of my life made any sense.

Sometimes my shield was the only thing that helped me through all the years with homeschooling and tutors. Watching kids play outside my window in the park across the road without me. Hearing all those whispers every day at the library when I went to pick up my new books.

My shield reminded me of the things that were important to me, and friends were nowhere on that list. And now at Genius Academy, with six kids who were clearly incredibly close already, I would need it more than ever.

Grace nudged my shoulder with hers, startling me back to reality. I let out a long, slow breath, staring at the floor for a moment to hide the spark of heat in my cheeks from all those memories. Clenching my fists, I let my shield grow stronger around me.

When I looked up, Martha had crossed her arms, but her face remained soft. She probably pitied me. Or maybe she was sad for my mom, who would be stuck in jail now that her dumb kid couldn't hack a boarding school. It was third grade all over again, but this time, I couldn't go home. Not with Mom on the line. My arguments were ready: The orientation was insane, there was no way for me to know what was going on, what kind of a school puts kids in danger like that? I had to fight to stay to keep Mom safe, no matter what.

But one quick movement from Martha, gesturing to the chairs, and my mouth zipped shut.

"Sit," she said. "I'm afraid there has been an unfortunate incident."

I squirmed. Something about the way her dark eyes were boring into me made me feel as guilty as a dog that had stolen a pork chop.

"The death ray," she said, staring straight at me.

My ears rang, tinny and sharp. That was *not* what I was expecting to hear. The death ray's existence couldn't be a surprise to Martha. My heel tapped traitorously against the leg of my chair. Tell me I wasn't about to be expelled for inventing something revolutionary, when that was the very thing that got me sent here in the first place.

"What about it?" I made myself look her in the eye.

Everyone got quiet. The heat in my cheeks rose as they all turned to stare at me.

Martha blinked her heavily lidded eyes slowly. "It was locked in a secure location on this campus when you first arrived. And now . . ." She paused, scanning each of our faces. "It's gone."

Dun dun dunnn!

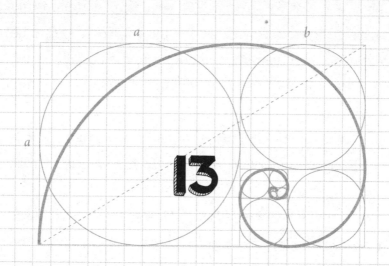

13

The air conditioning whirred, and for a second I didn't know what to say. The news was a punch to the gut, but not the one I'd been expecting.

I went with my first question. "This isn't about you kicking me out of here?" I asked. "For nearly drowning everyone and freaking out?"

Martha's eyebrows lifted. "Of course not. Don't be ridiculous. You relayed Geoffrey's hint to the rest of the team and worked together to get out of the cage in plenty of time. There's no reason to expel you for that."

I sank back in my chair. I wasn't sure whether I should be relieved or disappointed. *Plenty* of time wasn't exactly accurate—it'd been more like a few meager milliseconds—but I wasn't about to argue with her.

"Wait, wait," Grace interrupted. The look she gave me was laser sharp. "You're telling me you built a *death ray*? And brought it here?"

I tried to keep my voice steady. "I made it, yes," I said. "And they *made* me bring it here!" I pointed to Martha. Pickles hopped from my shoulder and ran toward her, as if to prove my point. "I couldn't exactly keep it at home with my mother! Martha, isn't there any way we could talk about this . . ." I looked to the others, who were also quietly staring back at me, their eyes full of curiosity. ". . . alone?"

Martha frowned. "These are your fellow students, Ms. Tesla. It's important you learn to work together. Vitally important."

I squirmed. There was that baloney about friendship and working together again. I crossed my arms hard across my chest and didn't respond.

Martha continued. "The agents who transported you here brought the death ray along for safekeeping," she said. "Usually, our security system runs twenty-four hours a day, seven days a week, without any interruptions. But for one minute and forty-three seconds this morning, our system was compromised. Shut off from the inside. And as I'm sure you can imagine, it could be catastrophic if Ms. Tesla's technology has fallen into the wrong hands."

I stared at my feet. My shoelaces were undone, tangled in a mess under my heel. It wasn't exactly my fault that someone had stolen the death ray. I mean, I wouldn't have built the thing if I thought someone would ever find out about it.

"From the *inside*?" I asked. "Doesn't that mean it was someone who works here?" I bit my lip. I didn't want to outright accuse someone at the academy, but I couldn't be the only one thinking about the possibility.

"Academy officials must pass the highest security clearances to work here," Martha said. "We have had a small turnover of security agents in recent months, and I'm working as quickly as I can to assess if they were involved in this incident. But again, that's highly unlikely."

"Unlikely doesn't mean impossible," I said, thinking of my own experience in my lab. Lots of research told me that my death ray was *unlikely* to work, and look how that turned out. "Unlikely just means it's a challenge."

"Fair point," Martha said. "In the meantime, we must exhaust all avenues."

The sandy-haired boy cleared his throat. "Leo, remember?" he introduced himself again. His damp hair settling over his eyes made him look like a shaggy golden retriever. "So, this death ray," he said. "I assume it's a particle beam weapon? Handheld, with a trigger?"

"Uh. Yeah," I said. I blinked at him. It wasn't every day someone guessed how my inventions worked. At least, they weren't usually right.

"Cool," he said. "I don't suppose you built some sort of transponder in it? So that we can track it?" he asked.

"No." I shook my head and my face got hot. "I didn't think I'd need one."

I could see now that not adding a tracker was an idiot

move. But how was I supposed to know that someone would try to steal something that I was going to keep secret in the first place? I didn't want them to think I was some careless dummy.

"None of my inventions have ever been stolen or gone missing before. Usually because no one even *knows* about them."

"Nobody thinks it's your fault, Nikki," said the blonde. Charlie. Her freckles jumped as she scrunched her nose. "You had no way of knowing anyone would ever find out about it, or that it would wind up here."

"Charlie's right," said the tall guy. "So what do we do to find this thing? What information do we have to go on? We can leave right away. Tonight, even."

I gawked around the half circle of chairs, then back at Martha. Her mouth was pinched together, but a small smile was growing on her face.

"What do you mean 'leave right away'?" I demanded. "Why is it on us to track it down? Don't you have some fancy security team that can do it? You know, go over video footage or surveillance or something? Why is this on us?"

Everyone went silent. Finally, Charlie spoke. "What is it you reckon we do here, Nikki?" she asked.

"I don't know," I said, shrugging. "Study? We are *geniuses* after all. I was told there would be a laboratory, for starters."

Mary grinned and nudged Leo. "Told you," she said. "She's got no idea."

"No idea about *what* exactly?" I said. My chest tightened and my voice was strained. "If you don't like me, go right ahead and say it! You don't need to talk about me like I'm not even in the room."

"Whoa, whoa!" Grace held up her hands. "No need for the drama here. Mary is just commenting on the nature of the academy, that's all."

Mary grinned. "You have to admit, it's a big plot twist."

"What do you mean?" I said. "Just tell me already. What is this place?"

I asked the question, but already the answer swirled in my head. Maybe I'd known the minute I saw the scroll listing all of those classes. *Advanced Lock Picking. Introduction to World Languages. Counterintelligence . . .*

Could Genius Academy be hiding something about its students?

The kids all exchanged glances, but it was Mo—the bearish guy with spiky black hair—who finally cleared his throat and spoke his first words to me since we'd met in the cage.

"Nikki." His voice was soft, like a lullaby. "This is Genius Academy."

I gave him a "so what?" look.

He glanced at Martha nervously before answering. "We save the world."

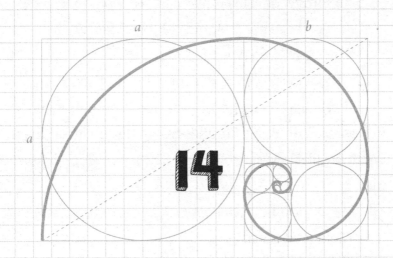

Are you still with me? This is probably a good time to stop and say holy ███████! The censors will probably black that out, too, but seriously. Can you believe it? I sure couldn't.

"What are you saying exactly?" I asked. I held my breath, suddenly afraid to disturb anything in the room.

"You know how in the X-Men, there's a secret school full of mutants that goes out and saves everyone when trouble strikes?" Grace said.

"*Yeaaah . . .*" I said. My memory took me back to the men in suits sitting in my living room. They knew I read X-Men comics to get through second grade. Did Grace and the others know, too?

She shrugged. "This is like that."

"Except we're not mutants," Mary added.

"Obviously," Leo piped in.

"Is it obvious?" Mo said, scratching his head.

I had to agree with him. Seven geniuses and a woman in a pantsuit all sitting around a room discussing a stolen death ray like it was no big deal? Sure, nothing odd about that.

"Maybe a little ... *mutant-ish*," Leo admitted, smirking. "Mutant adjacent."

"Think about it," Grace continued, waving off the comments from the others. "We're all geniuses, so we can figure stuff out a lot easier than most people. Do you remember what was on the top of the brochure when you came here? The only rule for Genius Academy?"

I shook my head. "I didn't get a brochure," I said. I was lying. I had gotten one, but I was so ticked off about them trying to blindfold me in the backseat that I threw it out the car window on the way here in a fit of annoyance. Looking back, that wasn't my best idea.

"*Uti bonum animum tuum,*" the tall kid said.

I translated the Latin in my head. "Use your mind for good."

"That's right," Martha said. She'd been quietly watching us—watching *me*—as everyone dropped this X-Men business on me. "Genius Academy prides itself on students who work tirelessly, efficiently, and brilliantly to accomplish whatever task is set before them. We'd like for you to join us, Ms. Tesla. It's why we invited you here. Not to punish you. To encourage you. You passed your initiation with flying colors."

Grace snorted. "Well, not *flying* colors," she said. "Hovering colors, maybe. Floating hues." She gave me a tiny smile.

I recoiled, gripping my arms tighter around me. Something about Grace gave me the distinct feeling of being . . . *exposed*. Like she could see right into my heart with those sharp eyes. I called Pickles over, eager to feel her protective, familiar fur on my neck.

She sighed. "Maybe we should take a second and introduce ourselves properly. You know, now that you're really in this."

A shiver zipped through me. Was I really in this?

"Good idea," Martha said. "Ms. Tesla, allow me. Every student at Genius Academy is skilled in several areas that help keep our operation afloat. Of course, we contain multitudes, so we are all much greater than the sum of our parts."

"Walt Whitman!" Mary chimed in.

I blinked at her. "Huh?"

She beamed. "'I contain multitudes.' That quote. It's from Walt Whitman."

"Oh . . . *kay* . . ." I said.

Grace clapped her hands together once. "Welp, that's Mary for you, Tesla. Mary Shelley is our resident writer. She's a genius when it comes to all things communication, as well as a whiz in chemistry, forensics, and divination."

"Divination?" I repeated. "As in, seeing the future?" I gawked at Mary, who merely batted her eyelashes back at me. I envisioned her waving her hands over a crystal ball, or deciphering the future in splotches of tea leaves.

"Not the way you think," Grace clarified. "Mary can often tell what people are going to do based on logic and intuition. Like any great writer, she anticipates plot twists."

Mary winked at me. "No crystal balls, I promise. I also make a mean macaroni and cheese," she said. Martha looked on with amusement. I made a mental note to stay away from Mary. I didn't need her snooping around my brain and figuring out the real reason why I was here.

"I'll go next." This time it was the tall kid who spoke. "You already know me. My name's Albert Einstein, but please call me Bert. Statistically Albert is a name for old men who eat prunes." His fingers drummed incessantly on his knee. "I'm into physics, math, philosophy . . . you know. That kind of thing. And I do not eat prunes."

A loud snore erupted beside me. *"Yawn,"* the little blonde girl said. "Math schmath. Ignore him. I'm Charlotte Darwin. Charlie to my friends. Naturalist. Scientist. Biologist. Geologist. Lots of 'ists,' really. If you ever find any wildlife around this place, let me know because they've probably escaped from my lab. Mo, you're up!"

Mo opened and closed his mouth, clearly deciding what he wanted to say. Big and burly, everything about him was slower than the others, even the way he spoke. He reminded me of a bear waking from hibernation. "I'm Adam Mozart. Most people call me Mo. I'm a musician and mathematician. I usually run the sound systems and security with Bert."

There was a long pause as I waited for him to continue, but instead he dug into his pocket. Pulling out a peppermint, he quietly untwisted the wrapper and popped the candy into his mouth.

"What?" he asked, peering at the others. The candy made his cheek puff out. Now he looked like a bear with a mouth full of food. "I'm done."

"Right," I said. I took a moment to scan everyone in the group, trying to commit their names to memory.

Charlie, the mouse, with the English accent. Mo, big guy who liked math and music. Grace, clearly the leader, respected by everyone. Bert, tall, lanky computer nerd who didn't eat prunes. Mary, the writer, who always had a smile for me. When I got to Leo, the bewilderment on my face must have been coming through loud and clear. Luckily, he took pity on me in the awkward situation.

"Well said, big guy. Mo's a man of few words." Leo patted Mo on the shoulder and playfully rolled his eyes at me. I waited for him to introduce himself, but Bert jumped in.

"Could we hurry this along?" His fingers now drummed double time. "We've got a death ray on the loose, and a whole world to cover in order to find it. Let's wrap up the intros, yeah?"

Martha nodded. "Agreed. Ms. Tesla, I know you'll get to know everybody all in due course. For now, it's crucial that we get to work. I'm sorry for throwing you into the deep end like this, but extreme times call for extreme measures."

Charlie snorted. "Deep end! Hah! Because of the pool! *Classic* Martha."

I whirled around to stare at her. "Seriously? Aren't we a little waterlogged to be joking about that?"

Grace stood up. "Okay, enough bickering." She made a "hurry it up" gesture with her hands. "Long story short, we're all geniuses; *yadda yadda yadda*, we save the world. Good for now?"

"Hold up," I said. "Save the world from *what*?" My brain sputtered, packed too full with new information. Genius Academy. All these weird kids. X-Men. For a group of kids meant to be geniuses, I was starting to feel like a giant, confused dummy. I still couldn't get the idea of skintight unitards and capes out of my head.

Martha lifted her hands grandly. "All crimes, plots, and heists, global or domestic, that threaten our way of life. We're the good guys, Nikki." She cleared her throat and walked around to the other side of her desk. "And right now, the good guys need to find that death ray. Before the worst happens."

"So someone with bad intentions has my death ray right now," I said, getting myself up to speed. "We have no idea who it is, and somehow we're in charge of getting it back? How exactly are we supposed to do that?"

"This is Genius Academy, after all," Martha said. "You *outthink* the enemy. But we don't have much to go on. A single clue that was recovered from the armory. The only thing missing was Nikki's death ray."

She reached behind her and lifted up a small plastic bag, the kind you'd pack your sandwich in for lunch. Inside the bag was a tiny slip of paper. "I'll show you everything we've got."

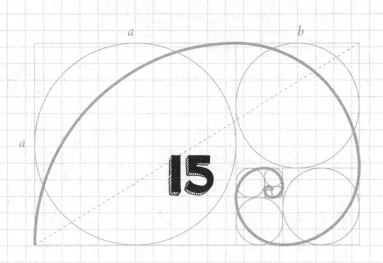

If you're expecting some big moment here, so was I. Maybe a ransom note made with creepy magazine clippings? Or a selfie of the dastardly thief with a nasty message scrawled out for us? But all we had to go on was a tiny slip of torn paper.

She set the paper down on the desk. "It's been dusted for prints, but we haven't been able to find anything useful yet. All we have is two words."

Leo picked up the note, squinting at the messy writing. "Find Atlas," he read aloud. For a moment, I wanted to interrupt everyone and ask him what his genius skill was—he was the last piece of the geek squad puzzle, and something about his easy smile in this unfamiliar

place made me feel the teensiest bit better—but I couldn't think of a way to ask without feeling like a total weirdo.

Get with the program, Tesla. I shook my head to clear it and stepped forward to check out the paper.

Everyone leaned forward to examine it, and I could practically hear the genius gears in their heads whirring. My own brain was trying to connect the dots, too. Whoever had written the message had *my* death ray. And if they did something horrible with it, I'd be the one to blame. A tight curl of fear snaked up my spine.

"Find a world atlas, maybe?" Charlie suggested. She peeked her head over Grace's shoulder. "There are dozens of them in the library. The thief could have left a clue in one of them to send us on a wild turkey chase."

"Goose," Mary corrected.

"Whatever," Charlie said, waving her hand. "A feral fowl of undesignated nature, then."

"Wait," Mary said. "Does anyone else think it's a little weird that we even *have* this clue? I mean, it's not much to go on. Looks like part of a to-do list to me. But it also kind of looks like someone left it here on purpose. This is an instruction, right? What if it's a trap?"

Now, that idea made my skin prickle. If Mary was an expert on what people were plotting, maybe she was right about the note?

"I think that we need to be careful here," she continued. "What are the odds that someone got through the academy's entire security system without a hitch, yet *accidentally* left a clue like this behind?"

"About four million to one, by my count," Bert said. He reached over above the rest of us to scoop up the bag containing the note. Holding it to the light, he narrowed his eyes. "I bet we were meant to find this clue. Presence of evidence in this case is signal of intention."

"Right," Grace said. "But it's still all we have to go on. So even if we anticipate a trap, we still need to move forward."

"I agree," Martha said.

I scanned her face for any signs of deception. It *was* weird that the piece of paper was left behind for us to find. Too coincidental.

"Find Atlas..." Charlie repeated. There was a far-away look in her eyes. "Atlas. *Atlas*."

Leo lifted his hand triumphantly. "That's it!"

We dodged out of his way as he raced over to a computer screen at the side of the room and began typing frantically. A web browser popped up, projecting onto the wall beside us. This was no regular office space; the tech was state-of-the-art. The hair stood up on the back of my neck as I watched the screens flash before me.

"What if it isn't find *an* atlas?" Leo explained. "What if we need to find Atlas! *The* Atlas. Look. In the note, it's capitalized."

"The Titan?" Grace said, crossing over to him. "What was his deal again? Something about a fight with Zeus?"

I thought back to lessons with my Greek tutor, but nothing jumped out at me. Mythology was not one of the areas I was anywhere near a genius in.

Mary began pacing. She twirled a damp piece of hair with her finger as she spoke. "The Titans lost a war with the Gods, and Zeus made Atlas hold up the sky on his shoulders to punish him. What does that have to do with the death ray? Is there some modern-day Atlas that the thief is looking for?"

"The *Farnese Atlas*," Leo said. "This has to be it." He clicked the keyboard and an ancient graying statue of a naked man holding the earth on his shoulders popped on-screen. "It's a marble statue from the second century. This says it's seven feet tall, and the globe is over two feet in diameter. It's in the National Archaeological Museum in Naples, Italy. Maybe the thief is headed to this statue next. Or the statue itself could be a clue to why he wants the death ray in the first place."

I read the slip of paper again. If it was true that the thief's next move was to "find Atlas," then Leo's idea about the statue was a good one. But if we were being set up, the Atlas statue could mean trouble.

"I don't know, guys," I said. "What if this whole thing is a diversion? Like Mary said, it's pretty unlikely that we found the clue by accident. Whoever left it wanted us to find it."

A hush fell over the group. Nobody argued with me, and I could tell by the way their mouths were

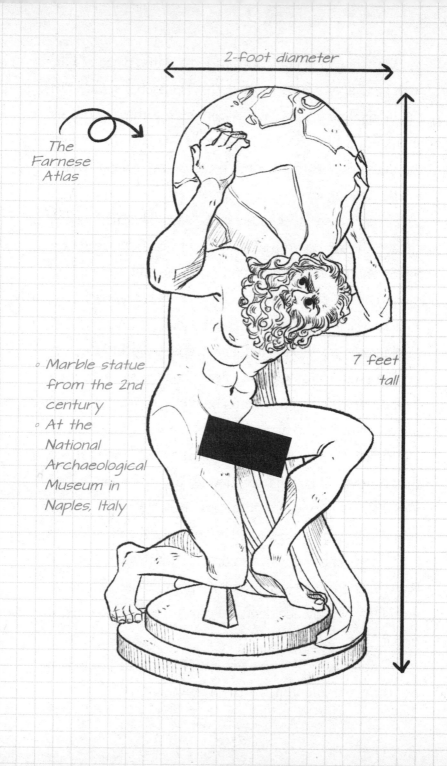

2-foot diameter

The Farnese Atlas

7 feet tall

- Marble statue from the 2nd century
- At the National Archaeological Museum in Naples, Italy

pinched tight that they understood the danger of pursuing Atlas.

Finally, Martha spoke. "What are our other options?"

Grace gripped the back of her chair. A grimace scrunched up her face. "We do nothing," she said. "We ignore the clue and wait to see what happens next." She turned to me. "And we cross our fingers that whoever took that death ray doesn't use it."

A weight settled into my stomach, unwilling to move. "Hoping nothing bad happens doesn't feel like the smart thing to do."

A hint of a smile appeared on Martha's face again. "I agree, Nikki. There are instances where doing nothing is the smartest plan. This does not appear to be one of those instances."

"We can try to figure out who left the clue," Mary said. "Leo, do you think you could run the note through the handwriting analysis app you made last year? It's a long shot, but if we cross-reference it to police databases, we might be able to find something."

"On it," Leo said. He grabbed a nearby stool and turned his back to us, his fingers racing across the keyboard in front of him. Small windows zipped across the screen, far too fast for me to read them all.

"What do we do until then?" I asked. The longer I thought about it, the harder it got to prevent awful scenarios from playing out in my imagination. My death ray didn't just obliterate people. It could also vaporize *any* material. Doors to bank vaults. Locked prisons. There wasn't any place on earth that was safe if someone wanted to use it. I tried to ignore the shadow of shame creeping over me.

"One wrong move and that death ray could go off," I said. "What if someone gets hurt?"

"Until we can ID the thief, we don't really have a choice," Grace said.

"So it's settled, then," Martha said. "I'll tell Marcus to fuel the jet. *Felicitazioni*, you're going to Italy."

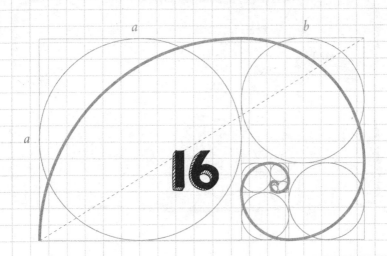

Here's the thing about Italy: Everywhere you look, there are statues of naked people. Naked people holding vases, naked people above fountains. Naked people—everywhere. It was *not* what I expected.

We flew to the city of Naples overnight on a red-eye flight, but instead of going to the airport and waiting in the security line for hours, the eight of us (that is, seven kids and one Pickles) simply went outside to the airstrip behind Genius Academy, where our very own private jet and Marcus, the pilot, were waiting for us.

Did you faint reading that?! That's right. Genius Academy has its *own* jet. Even Pickles was allowed to come with us. And here I thought having our own ice cream truck was cool. If I wasn't so freaked out about the

"saving the world" business, I might have been pretty stoked. Especially when I realized we didn't need to wear spandex onesies like the X-Men.

It took us seven hours to get to Naples, and when we touched down, Martha emailed us digital passes to the museum. I was glad I managed to sleep on the plane for a couple hours, because I was quickly learning that, to Martha, there was no such thing as rest. It was also the first chance I'd had to get my head around meeting everyone. Traveling to Italy was one thing, but traveling with a group of people you barely know? The questions about my inventions and experiments and even my favorite pizza toppings never stopped. The whole thing made me feel like I was being judged constantly, like they were all eager to get to know me and find out how I'd fit in with them.

Spoiler alert: I wouldn't. They could be as inviting and friendly as they wanted. Since they were geniuses, it was only a matter of time before they realized it. My plan was to find my death ray as fast as possible, and if I had to put up with them to do it, so be it. It also made me wonder: How many of the geniuses were here because men in suits had threatened *their* parents?

When we arrived at the museum, I scanned through a museum guide to find the statue we were looking for. "Atlas is to the left," I said, angling to peer over the crowd at the door. The place was packed, and I had to keep my feet firmly planted to stop people from jostling into me.

Keeping my hand tightly wrapped around the strap of my backpack—which contained a not-so-happy-to-be-trapped Pickles—I watched with curiosity as Grace made small talk with the ticket collector. The woman was clearly confused to see a group of kids traveling without a teacher, and grabbed the walkie-talkie on her hip. But Grace wasn't deterred. Smiling easily, she spoke quickly in Italian, gesturing and laughing. After a few minutes, she showed the collector our e-tickets, accompanied by a self-deprecating grin.

"Here we go," Grace said, using her arms to herd the seven of us together to get our entrance guides. Once inside, she huddled us together. "I could tell the ticket collector was concerned we're here without a teacher. Everybody lay low. Be tourists, remember? We're on a school trip and our teacher happens to be in the bathroom the whole time," she instructed.

Be a tourist. Right. I could do that.

Looking Like a Tourist 101

totally and completely lost

stare at the ceiling for no reason

fanny pack at the ready

maps out the wazoo

comfortable shoes

I looked around, gawking at the incredible sight before me. The museum was beautiful, with sparkling marble floors and creamy white columns. A painted dome ceiling arched over us, and delicate paintings adorned every wall. My head swam with color palettes and brushstrokes. There were so many treasures, it was hard to know where to look first.

"Whoa, check this out." I stopped in front of a massive white sculpture of several naked dudes wrestling a bull.

"*The Farnese Bull,*" Mary said, sidling next to me. That was another thing I was quickly learning—all these kids were *excellent* at sneaking up on people. It was like they were all part cat. She looked down at the guide in her hand. "It's been in the museum collection since 1826 and is the largest sculpture recovered from antiquity."

"Wow, it's really . . . *marbleous.*" I cracked up at my own bad joke, then ducked my head in embarrassment. To my surprise, nobody scoffed or snickered at me. In fact, Charlie cackled from behind her camera.

"Hey," Leo said, nudging me with his elbow. "How did they cut the Roman Empire in half?"

I blinked at him, confused.

"With a pair of Caesars! *Heyo!*" He grinned, fully pleased with himself.

I snorted a laugh and gestured to all the statues surrounding us. "I bet a lot of people take that joke for *granite* . . ."

"Oh dear. It looks like Leo's finally met his horrible pun match," Bert muttered under his breath. "We can't handle *two* of these jokers, can we?"

"Yo," Grace interjected. "Don't get sidetracked. There's a reason we're here."

I stood straighter and kept moving, leaning in to whisper to Mary. "She's pretty bossy, isn't she?"

Mary nodded. "She is, but that's why we need her. Grace is a natural leader. She's been at Genius Academy longer than almost all of us. We all trust her."

"That's her skill," I realized aloud. Grace walked ahead of us with purpose, her head held high. Despite her skinny frame, grown adults stepped out of the way for her. There was no question she was confident, but the way she carried herself wasn't just assertive. She was *inviting*. The way she charmed the worried ticket collector. The way everyone at the academy looked to her first, for everything. How did she do that?

Mary cocked her head. "Oh, you mean from yesterday? Why she's at the academy? Yes. Grace is people savvy, all right."

"She's like a magnet," I said.

"It's true," Mary said. She looked at Grace with admiration. "She has this way about her. If she needs something, she gets it. She knows what makes people tick. I think that's why people let her lead. They *want* her to."

I chewed on that. I wasn't used to knowing other geniuses at all, but someone who was so *people* smart? That was like meeting an alien. I didn't want to admit it, but I liked Grace. I wanted to be someone like that, who felt okay in her own skin. She behaved with confidence, but wasn't too in your face about it. Maybe calling her bossy wasn't really fair. She was just . . . in charge. In fact, I was sort of surprised that I was getting along with everyone in the group so far. A question popped into my mind.

"Who's been at the academy the longest?"

"Leo," Mary said. "He was the school's first student. I think he was five years old."

I frowned. *Five?* That seemed so young to leave your parents and haul off to some weird boarding school for geniuses. All those years with Martha in her pantsuits, sneaking up on you. I couldn't imagine that. How had he turned out so normal? Mary read my mind.

"He was young, but he wasn't having a good time at school," she explained. "Even back in kindergarten, the other kids could tell something was different about him.

He was making flying machines and memorizing complex anatomy when everyone else was still eating their crayons."

I nodded, wondering if Leo was bullied like I was. He wasn't shy or awkward around the others at all, unlike me, who was clearly a giant, awkward weirdo even saying hello to new people. An *awkweirdo*.

"What's his deal?" I asked. I tried to frame the question like I was merely curious, and not secretly dying to know more about Leo. "You're a genius writer. Grace is a leader. What's Leo all about?"

She glanced back at him. He was poring over a guidebook with a pencil tucked behind his ear. His shaggy hair had fallen over his forehead again. "Leo's very special," she said. "He's a polymath. Art, mathematics, engineering. Even botany. Leo's good at everything and *amazing* at finding connections between different subjects."

I tried to watch him without staring. My head and heart were fighting each other. I wasn't used to being surrounded by such smart kids. It sort of freaked me out, like I wasn't *really* smart enough to be here. What if they realized it and kicked me out before I could help them find my death ray? I shook my head to banish the idea. *Shield up, Tesla. They don't matter. Focus on your death ray.*

"Don't worry," Mary said. "We need an inventor like you here, Nikki. You're one of us now."

I stiffened. "You seriously need to stop reading my mind." I glared at her. "Are you sure you're not some kind of psychic?"

She shrugged mysteriously. "I'm a writer," she said. "Writers read, you know. Body language speaks way louder than words. And *you* are an open book!"

"Is everyone keeping an eye out for anything suspicious?" Grace interrupted. She turned on her heel and walked backward for a second, facing us. "We don't know anything about whoever stole the death ray yet, so don't trust *anyone* here, all right?"

Back to business, the seven of us made our way down the busy hall, navigating through the throngs of tourists. I fell into step beside Mo, the only truly quiet one of the bunch. It was nice to have a moment to myself to take in the scenery while we walked. If I wasn't here to search for evidence about my missing death ray, I could spend ages nerding out over the different statues and pieces of art.

"Here he is," Leo said. He stopped in his tracks, pointed to the large statue in front of us, and tapped his guidebook.

Atlas looked like he did on the Internet. Muscles. Irritated to be holding the whole world on his shoulders. And yep, you guessed it—also naked. Apart from the nudity, I could relate to how he felt.

"What is it with these artists and being nude?" Bert asked. He frowned at the statue, clearly unimpressed. "Would it kill them to give Atlas a fig leaf? Or a pair of shorts? Even a Speedo would be better than nothing."

"European culture is much different than back home," Mary said. "They're more open about some things, like nudity. And Italian stories are full of passion and intrigue. You can see it in all their sculptures!"

"Bet there's some nude beaches around here, too. Studies show that Europeans are much more likely to go to nude beaches," Mo said, waggling his eyebrows.

"Eyes on the prize, guys," Grace said. "We better hurry it up. Look." Her eyes darted to a security guard lingering by the window, watching us. He had the telltale look of an adult who didn't want kids in his museum.

"We're here in the middle of the day on a Monday with no parents around. We need to wrap this up before our cover is blown. Statue experts." She shoved Mary and Leo toward Atlas for a closer look. "Do your thing."

I angled myself to get a better look at the security guard. He was still watching us with dark, judgmental eyes. Every few seconds, his feet shuffled a half step closer to us. The thing about having someone steal your death ray is that you start to think everyone is guilty.

"Wait, look at this," Mary said suddenly. She pored over the surface of the marble as close as she could without touching it. "There's something wrong with this sculpture."

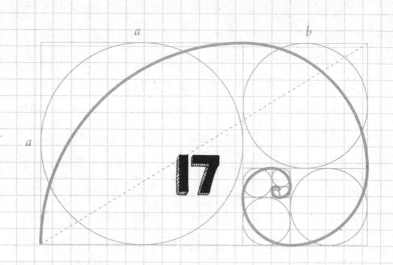

17

"What is it?" Leo asked.

Beside him, Grace took some pictures with her phone to make it look like we were regular students visiting the museum. Mary flashed a peace sign and posed like a tourist beside Atlas.

"Do you see these marks?" Bert asked. He pointed to Atlas's shoulder and leg.

"The white patches?" Charlie said. "It looks like some sort of chalk." She sniffed the air like she was trying to smell the statue without leaning close.

"It's called efflorescence," Bert said. "It happens when some stone surfaces get wet. The powder is a soluble salt. Look, it's everywhere, even on the floor." He peeked at the security guard, and when he saw the coast was clear,

Effloresence 101

How does it work?

white stuff

Cement + Air + Water = Effloresence + Evaporation

$Ca(OH)_2$ CO_2 H_2O $CaCO$ $2H_2O$

Effloresence is a white layer of salts that can occur on some stone surfaces. Here's how it works on cement!

swiped the floor near the statue with his fingertip. Lifting it to his mouth, he took a tiny lick. "Definitely efflorescence," he confirmed.

"There are reports that this museum is haunted," Mary said, pulling a magnifying glass from her bag. She began inspecting the white patches, while Grace and Charlie stood between her and the guard, acting as a wall. "Strange things happen at night here, and there are several claims that objects get moved or even disappear. Maybe a ghost had something to do with this."

"I don't think that ghosts leave fingerprints that need to be cleaned," Leo said. "But the museum's reputation for the mysterious movement of objects would be a perfect way to cover your tracks if you came here and *did* move something."

Bert posed for a fake photo, giving me bunny ears. "Why would our death ray thief want to come here and clean a statue?"

That didn't sound right to me. "What if he didn't clean it, but the museum staff did? It could be a coincidence."

Mo cleared his throat. "Uh, not sure if it matters, but did anyone notice there's no plaque for this statue?" He gestured to the rest of the room, where ornate plaques were displayed beside each work of art.

"Now, that's no coincidence," Mary said, narrowing her eyes. "I wonder where it went?"

Bert and I stepped back, scanning up and down the statue for more clues.

"So what?" Charlie asked. "The plaque is missing, and somehow cleaning the statue is connected to that?

What message is this thief trying to send us here?" She scratched her head.

A tinny beep interrupted us. Leo startled at the noise, reaching into his pocket quickly.

"Uh, guys?" Leo said. He stared at the screen of his phone. "I've got something here. The handwriting analysis app found a match. I know who took the death ray."

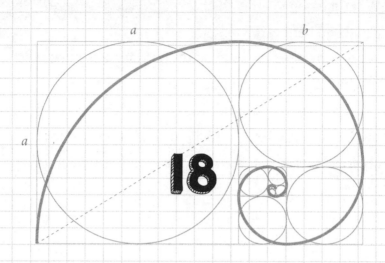

18

He held up his phone.

"Alexander Zarn," I read aloud. A small image of a tall, wiry man with icy blue eyes stared back at us. His hair was so blond it looked white, and there was an upturned sneer on his lips. The picture looked like it had been taken from security camera footage, somewhere in a bank or public building.

"Who the heck is that?" I asked. "I've never seen him before in my life." My shoulders drooped. I'd been hoping the culprit would turn out to be someone I knew, like a weird neighbor or mailman. Much better chances of finding them that way, right?

Bert planted himself on a bench and pulled his laptop out of his backpack. "We'll know soon enough."

"Albert's got this," Mary whispered to me. "He's cracked into every government database known to man. It usually takes him less than ten, nine, eight, seven, six . . ." She counted off on her fingers.

"Got it!" Bert said, beaming up at us. He narrowed his eyes at Mary for a moment. "And it's *Bert*," he clarified. "Not Albert. Note the distinct lack of prunes in my diet?"

Grace sighed. "The thief?" she reminded him, barely hiding her grin.

Bert blinked at her for a second before continuing. "Right. Thief." He looked down at his screen and read. "Alexander Zarn. Thirty-eight years old, from Zurich. Has been arrested several times on weapons charges and conspiracy. He was also recently busted for trying to break into a Swiss energy plant. The file says he was looking for electromagnets. Before that, he worked in cybersecurity for a bank."

A chill skipped along my spine. "Electromagnets," I said. "Did he get them?"

Bert nodded. "I think so," he said. "He got caught, but he jumped town and skipped his parole hearing. There's a warrant out for his arrest."

"Sounds like an all-around lovely chap," Charlie muttered. "Delightful."

"Who breaks into an energy plant when they can break into a bank instead? Isn't that a little counterproductive?" Mary asked.

"Someone who doesn't want money," Mo said quietly.

"Martha said our security was breached from the inside," Leo said. "Does anyone recognize him?"

Bert held up the laptop to give us all a closer look. After a few moments, everyone else shook their heads. "Nope," they said in unison.

"And you, Nikki?" Leo asked. "Have you seen this guy before?"

"I just got here, remember?" I took a better look at his picture and hoped for a flicker of recognition. Pale skin. Blond hair. Those icy bright eyes. Was there something familiar about him? "I don't think so," I said. "I've really only met Martha and Geoffrey so far. That's obviously not either of them."

"So nobody's seen this bloke," Charlie said. "But what do electromagnets and cybersecurity have to do with the Atlas statue? Whoever Alexander Zarn is, he left that note in our weapons vault."

"I have an idea," Grace said. She marched over to the security guard, dragging me with her. "We're going to find out about this statue once and for all."

"Ciao!" She lit up in a huge smile as we approached the guard. He didn't respond. The tag on his uniform said his name was Vincenzo, and there was a five o'clock shadow of scruff on his face. He looked like he'd much rather go for lunch break than be guarding a bunch of statues, if you ask me.

"My friend Sophie and I were wondering about this place. We're on a class trip." She pointed to where the rest of our team was waiting. "Has anything out of the ordinary happened in the past few days? And is there a reason that statue has no plaque?"

Vincenzo narrowed his eyes. "Why do you ask?"

Grace shrugged. "No biggie, just wondering. I read in the newspaper that *ghosts* haunt this museum. Is that true? Do you think they could cause a disturbance in here?" Her eyes darted to the sides and she gave her best impression of a spooked kid.

"As a matter of fact, we had to remove Atlas's plaque yesterday. Someone vandalized it." He spoke slowly, like he was testing us with every word he said.

"Really? How?"

I listened carefully, blocking out the sounds of tourists and cell phone camera clicks around us. This had to be Zarn's trail of evidence. Why vandalize a museum plaque?

"That's right," Vincenzo said. He took a step forward. "Someone got their filthy paws all over the statue, which meant it required cleaning. They also switched the Arctic and Antarctic Circles on the plaque's diagram."

I let out a tiny huff of annoyance. So Zarn had brought us all here to show us he'd messed with a statue? For what?

"Wow, that's too bad," Grace continued to chat breezily with the guard. "Are vandals like that common here? Did you happen to catch any of it on security footage?"

The guard worked his jaw, sending his thick neck muscles jumping. If I could tell he was suspicious of us now, Grace had to see it, too.

"Seems quite a coincidence you would ask a question like that right after the incident. Especially considering it wasn't reported. I've been standing here all day and nobody's noticed that missing plaque." And then, the words I'd been dreading. "What school did you say you were with?"

Uh-oh.

Grace was unrattled. "Lincoln Middle School, in Maine."

"Is that so? Would you mind pointing your teacher out to me? I'd love to make sure everyone signs the guestbook…"

How to Lie: A Crash Course in Deception Tips by Grace O'Malley

stand up tall

shoulders back

chin up

don't fidget with your hands

use as few words as possible

pretend you own the building you're standing in

IMPORTANT: Security guards can smell fear.

"Sure," Grace said, spinning around. She took a scan of the room and turned back to Vincenzo. "Looks like she went to the bathroom. Ms. Markham isn't feeling too well today. Jet lag. I think she had some bad chicken on the plane, too. Thanks, though!"

Grace wheeled us away back to the statue, gripping my arm tight. "Did you know that Lincoln is the most popular school name in America, *Sophie*?" she said.

"You're going to get us caught!" I warned.

"He'd already made us." She waved her hand dismissively. When we reached the others, they all perked up to listen. "Jackpot, guys. It looks like ol' Atlas here had his plaque vandalized yesterday. They had to clean him, so that explains the other marks. I would have gotten more, but we were running out of time with Vincenzo back there." She gestured over her shoulder.

"Looks like you overestimated the time you had," Leo said. He tightened the straps of his backpack against his chest and his eyes darted to the exits. "We've got company."

I turned on my heel and gasped. I didn't have a lot of experience with the whole "blend in with tourists so you can inspect a statue" thing, but I was pretty sure that three men stomping their way toward you with armed security guards at their sides was *not* a good thing.

Whatever had happened with the statue, these guys thought *we* had done it.

"Why did you ask something so specific? All you did was make him think *we* had something to do with it!" Mary said, cracking her knuckles.

"Sometimes you don't have time to play games. You need answers. We've got a missing death ray, remember?" Grace said. "Nikki,"—she turned to me—"how fast are you? Ever run on Track and Field Day or anything?"

"Uh, homeschooled, remember?" I said. The guards were beelining toward us, with a museum manager at their side.

"Oh, it's really easy," she said. "Left foot, right foot, move 'em as fast as you can." She clapped me on the back. "Rendezvous at the pizzeria three blocks away after you lose them. Time to *run!*"

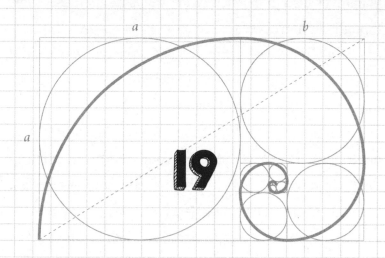

Unbelievable.

My first trip to a foreign country, and I was going to spend it running from security guards.

"Split up!" Leo yelled.

I fumbled for a moment, unsure of what direction to run. I'd always heard the phrase "run for your lives," but I'd never actually done it before. The others must have, because they split off in an exact burst pattern, with Charlie and Leo moving the fastest. Calculating the odds in a split second, I decided my best chance of escape was to my right, through a group of tourists by the bathroom, then under the rope partition out the front door.

What if they caught me? What if they thought I

belonged to some international ring of museum vandals? I panted hard, ducking around tourists and visitors, nearly plowing directly into an old man drawing on a huge sketchpad on his knee. *Get it together, Tesla. This is exactly like running at the park! A park with priceless art!*

"Sorry!" I yelped, dodging yet another selfie stick hoisted in the air, which nearly took my eye out.

Rounding the corner by the bathroom, the exit loomed in front of me. I shifted on toes and prepared to launch myself under the corded red rope to the outside world. I hoped that Pickles was hanging on tight inside my bag. My feet slipped on the white floor, squeaking up a storm. The open air and blue sky were the only things I needed to focus on.

I calculated the angle. I needed to slide out the door without crashing into the sides. Knowing the math was one thing, but getting my body to actually *do* it was another. I should have pushed Mom harder for a PE tutor at home.

Sliding like I was diving for home base, I landed hard on my elbow and thigh. I sailed under the rope, skidding out the door on my legs and butt.

For a second, I was pretty darn proud of myself. I'd escaped! I had a bruised butt and road rash to show for it, but there was no sign of any guards or angry museum

workers. The day was bright and sunny, making it hard to see without sunglasses. I couldn't spot the others.

"You okay in there?" I reached back and gave my backpack a quick poke. Pickles ignored me, probably peeved about the ruckus. I'd owe her extra fries today, for sure.

"Pizzeria," I reminded myself. "Find the pizzeria."

I shoved off the ground and hauled myself up. Where was the pizzeria again?

Follow your nose, my gut said. Sniffing the air, I tried to catch a whiff of pizza dough and cheese. No such luck. Then I spotted a couple walking hand in hand, each stuffing their face with a cheesy, gooey pizza slice. They were walking toward me, away from a side street tucked behind some flower planters by a small café. Grace had said the pizzeria was three blocks away.

Gotcha.

I rushed down the side street, keeping my eyes open for more signs of pizza. The smell of tomato sauce and cheese began to waft in the air—I was getting closer. For the first time since arriving in Italy, I felt like Genius Academy wasn't the worst thing to ever happen to me. I was free and running away from security guards in Italy! It was like I was starring in my own action movie, racing at top speed down a cobblestone street with foreign police left in my wake. I was practically a superstar!

That lasted about five seconds.

As I turned on my heel to race down the final block, I crash-landed into a fountain and flipped headfirst into the water like a demented synchronized diver.

Shoooooot.

Okay, keep moving, I told myself. Dripping wet, I sloshed out of the fountain, ignoring the stares around me.

"Nothing to see here," I mumbled in Italian. Even the naked stone lady on *top* of the fountain was judging me, piercing me with her ancient eyes. Well, she was the naked one, so she had a lot of nerve.

To top off my incredibly bad luck, the hand that helped me out of the fountain belonged to an Italian police officer.

"*Scusa, signorina,*" he said, eyeing the water like he was unsure whether he should come in after me. Probably didn't want to ruin his shoes. I knew enough Italian to know that he was trying to help. But I also knew from the look in his eye that he was Capital Not Pleased.

"Hi," I said feebly. When he realized I spoke English, his lips smooshed together in a tight line.

"Would you care to explain to me where you're running?" he said. His accent was thick, but there was no mistaking his words.

"Uh, I really had to pee?"

I wished I had Grace's silver tongue. No wonder she was the leader. Leaders needed to *lie*. My muscles tensed as I hoisted my wet backpack higher on my shoulder, and a shiver of doubt rippled through me. My backpack seemed lighter than it should be. No squeaks or squeals chattered away inside it.

Something was wrong.

I moved without thinking. "No!" My voice caught in my throat as I dropped to my knees. The officer could wait. Frantic, I opened my backpack and rooted around, yanking out the spare T-shirt, notebook, and change purse.

No Pickles.

I gave the backpack another quick shake, desperate for a flash of familiar fur or angry chatter. But there was nothing.

pigeon feather

notebook

spark plug

Notes!

NO Pickles!!!

My chin began to tremble and I turned in place, scanning the area at lightning speed. "Pickles!" I shouted. Had she somehow escaped my backpack in the museum? Or run off when I'd skidded to the ground? *"Pickles!"*

A harsh, dry ache began to grow in the back of my throat. My best friend. I'd completely *lost* my very best friend. She was alone and defenseless in a foreign country because of me. "Oh, Pickles," I whispered. "I'm so sorry." I pictured her terrified, darting and dodging in between the legs of strangers as she tried to find me. We hadn't been separated since I first brought her home from the animal shelter as a kit. Tears began to well up in my eyes, and my vision began go all swimmy.

I could tell the officer wanted to console me but had no idea why I was so upset about pickles. Then the walkie-talkie on his hip chirped in Italian. I caught the words "museum" and "band of vandals." I tried to dart away, but he caught me by the arm. That's when I spotted Charlie and Leo peeking out from an alleyway a few yards away. Only the tops of their heads and saucer-wide eyes were visible, but I shot them a panicked look anyway. They *had* to help me. I desperately wanted to yell at them to split up and go search for Pickles. Well, as soon as they got me out of this mess.

"I'm sorry, miss," the officer said. "You're going to have to come with me."

I coughed, pretending like I was getting some fountain water from my lungs. Really, I was stalling for time and edging closer to Charlie and Leo's alley. Any minute now, they would cause a distraction so I'd have a chance to run away.

Any.

Minute.

The officer started to grab me by the elbow and steer me away.

Charlie and Leo didn't move. They didn't yell out. They didn't do anything. Instead, they ducked back around the corner.

My stomach bottomed out and disbelief hit me like a wave. They'd *left* me. I shuffled alongside the officer, leaving a soppy wet trail on the cobblestones under my feet.

It was official. My best friend was missing. I was in police custody. And I'd been in Italy for less than two hours and was already a wanted criminal.

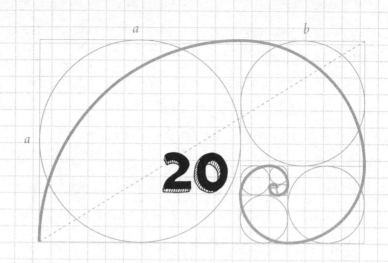

20

Did you know that "police headquarters" in Italian is *Palazzo della Questura*?

Now you do.

The only time I'd seen the inside of a police station was when Mom let me binge watch *Law & Order* when I got the flu. I was expecting lots of lights shining into my eyes, being forcefully interrogated, and coffee in paper cups. You know, cop stuff. I wanted to be prepared for anything they would throw at me, but my stomach lurched when I saw the tiny room and silver table they sat me at.

"Non ricevo una telefonata?" I asked, mimicking holding a telephone to my ear. I was pretty sure in America, people were entitled to a phone call so they could call their moms or rat out their friends.

Of course, this wasn't America. This was Italy. Land of the naked statues and overly suspicious museum guards.

The officer cocked his eyebrow without responding, then stepped out of the room. The sinking feeling in my stomach was getting worse by the second. I felt like a drowned rat. Tired. Reeking of stale fountain water. Pickles was alone, probably scared out of her little ferret mind. And after smelling all that pizza, I was hungry enough to eat a whole Italian bakery's worth of cannoli. I still couldn't believe that Grace and everyone else had left me when things got rough.

I was a colossal idiot. That was the truth, and it hurt worse than any of the bruises I had from my attempted escape. The minute I saw Leo and Charlie watching from the alleyway? I'd thought I was safe. I *knew* they would do something to get me out of there. At least, I thought I knew. That was the Genius Academy way, wasn't it? I'd let my shield evaporate for half a second and look where it got me. How stupid could I have been? Falling for all their talk about friends and teamwork.

I ran my fingernail over the cloudy surface of the steel table in front of me, hot embarrassment spreading through my chest. I kept reaching for Pickles, then remembering she was gone, and feeling completely exposed without her. My own defeated reflection in the table's shiny surface looked too much like my mother, and in a heartbeat, I was back outside that classroom, eavesdropping on her and my teacher.

Despite our best attempts, Nikki has a hard time making friends.

Nikki doesn't fit in well with her peers.

Nikki doesn't fit in, period.

I could solve the most complex equations out there, and invent things that didn't exist, but I was still learning that Nikki plus friends never equaled a positive outcome. They'd taken off within seconds, ready to ditch me the first chance they got. All six of them were probably together right now, telling Martha how easily I'd been caught. Waves of panic morphed into shame, choking me.

I'd totally fallen for it. They were no different than the kids at my old schools. They didn't really want to be friends with me. The equation was never wrong.

Grinding my teeth, I covered my dirty reflection with my hands and willed myself to sit taller. Eyes up. Back straight. I may have been on my own, but I was good at that. I could handle one Italian police officer.

"Would you mind telling me your name, please?" The officer entered the room, interrupting my mental ranting.

I thought about telling him everything. About Genius Academy, and how they'd dragged me here and let me get hauled away by the police. How it *wasn't* my idea to investigate the statue. Maybe then he would let me go, and I could begin my search for Pickles.

But there were two problems with that plan, and they both hit me like an atomic blast from a well-designed bomb.

1. My death ray. No matter who had left me behind, my death ray was still in the hands of a thief. And I

couldn't let this Alexander Zarn get away with it. It's not like there's ever an *innocent* reason to steal a death ray.

2. *Mom*. The only reason she wasn't in jail was because I'd agreed to go to Genius Academy. If I spilled the beans on them, there was no way they'd care what happened to her. *Especially* if I sold them out to the Italian police.

There was no way out. This equation only had one answer.

I had to lie.

More importantly, I had to do it *well*.

Weighing the options, I decided that my best option was to play dumb. I was going let someone else do the lying for me.

I opened my mouth and went for it. "My name is Nemo and I can't find my father."

The officer blinked. His hand was hovering over his notepad. "Your name is . . . Nemo," he repeated. Already I could tell by the look on his face that it wasn't the first lie he'd heard all day.

"Yep," I continued, holding my head higher. I needed to double down on the lie now before I talked myself out of it. "I was swimming near some coral and *boom*, some huge net scooped me up. When I woke up, I was in this fish tank at a dentist's office. And whoa! Let me tell you, that was terrifying! But I made some friends. This one angelfish really saved my butt, and now I'm out of there, but I still can't find my dad. Do you think you could help me?"

I blinked innocently, ignoring the rumble in my stomach. He either thought I was messing with him, or completely out of my mind.

I hoped he went with the second one.

He set his pen down. "You're being held for questioning on suspicion of vandalizing a priceless artifact and you're quoting *Finding Nemo*? That's my daughter's favorite movie, you know."

I nodded, buying myself more time. If I could keep him talking, maybe I could think of a way out of this place. "Technically I'm not quoting. I'm *referencing*. It's one of my mom's favorites, too."

His face softened. But not enough to call the whole thing off and let me go, that was for sure. "Would you please tell me your real name? That way I can get ahold of your parents."

A laugh caught in my throat. Tell my mother I was in Italy investigating my stolen death ray, when I was supposed to be playing badminton with other nerds at boarding school? Teaching calculus to goats would go over better.

"The six other kids with you," he said. "Are they school friends of yours? Do you know them well?"

I drummed my fingers on my knees. I didn't want to talk about the abandoners. "Nope."

Above me, something thumped in the ceiling.

The officer's mustache twitched at the noise. He peered up in time to catch the grungy tile shift slightly. Someone—or something—was moving slowly through the ducts over our heads. His hand moved to his gun, and his eyes darted back to me.

"What the . . ." he said. He leaped back and gestured for me to remain still.

A small bag dropped to the desk in front of me. A tiny thing, half the size of a dollar bill. Foam earplugs wrapped in plastic. A sticky note was attached to them.

Put these in. –G.O.

G.O.?

Grace O'Malley?

I moved without thinking. I had no idea what the earplugs were for, but I didn't want to risk ignoring the note.

A mix of panic and overwhelming joy surged through me. The Genius Academy kids *hadn't* left me! They were in the building right now!

"Don't *move*!" the officer yelled at the ceiling. "We've been breached!" he said into the radio on his shoulder. "I repeat, we've been breached!"

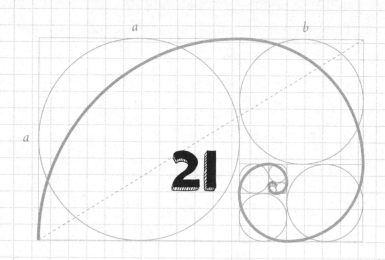

21

Earplugs. *Go!*

I had enough time to rip open the package and stuff the earplugs into my ears before the building started to shake. At first, the rumbling seemed like an earthquake, or maybe construction outside the police station. But when the officer clutched his ears and fell to his knees, I figured it out. It was *sound* that was causing the vibration. Thumping, screeching, vibrating sound that made my heart throb like it was going to bounce right out of my chest. Like I was at a rock concert cranked up to full volume, sitting on the biggest amplifier in the world.

Mo's legs appeared through the hole in the ceiling, then he dropped onto the silver table. For a big guy, he was surprisingly agile. Beads of sweat dripped down his face, and he was covered in chalky white dust from the vents above. Bright yellow earplugs stuck out of his ears. He hopped to the ground and gestured for me to follow him without saying a word.

We were only a couple of feet away from the cop, but he couldn't wrench his hands from his ears to grab either one of us. I would have felt bad for him—he was only doing his job, after all—but the adrenaline in my body wouldn't let me stop long enough to feel anything else. This was my only chance out of there and I wasn't going to waste it.

As we sprinted out of the room, I noticed we were the only ones in the building moving around normally. Everyone else was ducked into a fetal position, holding their ears. We raced down the hallway, past reception, and right out the front door.

"This way!" Mo yelled, yanking me down the street. With the earplugs still stuck firmly in my ears, the echoes of that raucous sound replayed in my head, and the city seemed to dance along with it. Bakers selling flour-dusted loaves of bread. Women in swishy skirts and heels, clutching their boyfriends' arms as they walked. Businessmen in tight-fitting suits sipping cappuccinos on patios. Mo and I wound around all of them, darting through the maze of streets. Somehow, he knew where he was going. He didn't make a wrong turn or stumble once.

When he jogged to a stop and held open a café door for me, I had to lean over to catch my breath and take out my earplugs. Who knew being a genius was so *physical*? I panted and tested my auditory cognition, snapping my fingers next to my ears. I could hear. And if I wasn't sure, the loud chorus of whoops and cheers that hit me when I stepped inside the café confirmed it.

I stared dumbfounded at the scene in front of me.

The whole team was crowded around an extralarge table, with a spread of food and drinks in front of them. The smell of freshly baked dough and cheese swirled around me. They were smiling—*every* one of them—happy to see me.

"You made it!" Grace yelled. She lifted her fork—there looked to be something chocolatey on it—and hooted. Leo, Charlie, Bert, and Mary all stood up and crowded around to give me a hug.

A million thoughts raced through my head. Calculating. Assessing. Could it be a trick? Some sort of setup? Leo's beaming face startled me out of my panicked thoughts. This didn't look like a joke to them. But if it wasn't a joke, did that mean they really were my friends? That equation didn't make sense either. I couldn't hold it all in.

"I thought you guys had left me for dead!" I shouted. Anger and relief balled together inside me. How could they let me think for even a *second* I was on my own back there?! My chest fluttered with excitement as I took in the amazing spread of food on the table.

"Leave you?" Grace handed me a slice of pizza and patted my back. "Genius Academy never leaves a man behind."

"Or woman!" Charlie said, her mouth full of what looked to be lasagna.

"Pull up a chair," Grace said. She squeezed closer to Leo to make room for me.

"I can't! I lost Pickles somewhere between the museum and fountain," I said, anxious to start the search. My heart fell once more saying the words out loud. "We need to spread out and find her. Nothing's stopping her from getting lost, or even being scooped up by some stranger. She's so friendly, you guys. I need to find her." I tried to keep my voice steady, but it was cracking dangerously.

Leo stood and gripped me by the shoulder. "It's okay," he said. "Look."

He leaned down and lifted the white linen table-cloth. At the foot of his chair, a small plate of cheese, breadsticks, and pepperoni slices was set out, with a folded napkin on the side. Pickles lay on her back with her hands up to her face, stuffing a pepperoni slice into her mouth.

"Oh my gosh," I said, melting to the floor. I scooped up Pickles in my arms and gave her the best hug I could summon. I couldn't stop the happy tears from streaming down my face. "You saved her!"

Pickles, who really just wanted to continue gorging herself, scurried out of my grip and back to her plate. Without thinking, I pulled Leo into a hug as well. "Thank you," I said. "You have no idea how much this means to me." I half sobbed in his ear.

Charlie cleared her throat and I realized I was still hugging Leo. Jumping away with a start, I turned to thank them all. "I owe you guys. Thanks," I said, trying to cover for how awkward I suddenly felt.

Mary grinned. "It was Charlie who noticed her," she explained. "She must have snuck out of your pack during our escape."

"No biggie," Charlie said. "I kept good care of her until we got here, and then Leo figured she needed a treat after everything she'd been through. Said there was no way you'd ever forgive us if you found Pickles upset."

Leo nodded. "It was the least we could do. Putting her through all that trouble. Pickles, I mean." His face turned slightly pink.

I plunked down and rolled my shoulders to unknot them while Pickles had the feast of her lifetime at our feet. Not only was I overjoyed to be free from the police, but the food smelled so good, I could barely concentrate. Instantly, my whole world revolved around carbs. They had ordered pizza, spaghetti, lasagna, and what looked to be every dessert on the menu, along with glasses of sparkling water and juices. I crammed a slice of pizza into my mouth and sank back against my chair in a deliriously happy cheese coma. *"Mmph, pho goodf!"*

"We needed to make sure we weren't followed," Grace said. "Once we met at the pizzeria, we hatched our little plan to break you out. You can thank Mo for the idea. Usually he specializes in classical music, but this time, he found us the perfect synthesized death metal. Bert piped it through the headquarters' PA system at a decibel that could stop the cops in their tracks. And Charlie used some mice to track the ventilation system and figure out where we could grab you. Pretty genius, right?"

"Really genius," I said. I swallowed my pizza and moved on to a pile of cannoli. Something about being chased by the cops really works up an appetite. "But how did you know which station I was at? There must be several in the city."

Leo reached and twirled the small pin on my shoulder, sending a quick thrill through me. My atom pin, from my first day at the academy. I didn't even realize I'd stuck it to my shirt. "Didn't Martha tell you?" My heart skipped a beat as he waggled his eyebrows at me. "Accessories are crucial to a good outfit."

I sucked in a breath, heat rising to my cheeks.

"There's a tracking chip in our pins," Mary explained. "We all have one. If one of us gets lost or in trouble, it's easy to find them."

"You're welcome," said Bert, tapping his laptop.

I twisted the pin, counting the electrons again. Carbon, with one electron for each kid at the academy. *Except for* me, I realized. I swallowed my mouthful of pizza and tried to act unfazed, but the food tasted oddly stale in my mouth now. The pin was a firm reminder of where I stood with the academy. Unproven, unknown. "What's next, then?" I mumbled between bites.

Grace wiped her mouth with a napkin, but before she could answer me, a low ringing sound vibrated.

"Hang on," she said. She swiped her phone with her finger and tapped it a couple of times. I could tell from the shadow that passed over her face that she had bad news.

"What is it?" Mary asked.

Grace set the phone down. "A text from Martha," she said. "We've got a problem."

"Was she mad about me getting caught?" I squirmed, pushing a chocolate strawberry around on my plate absently and braced for the worst. After the feast of bad luck I'd had today, I wasn't sure I could handle a side dish of guilt.

"No." Grace shook her head. "Bert, pull up Interpol's website on your laptop, would you?" A small crease appeared between her eyes.

Bert did as he was told. Clicking a few keys at warp speed, his face went pale.

"*No*," he said. He scratched his head in confusion and clicked the page again, refreshing it. "This can't be right."

Grace sighed. "So it's true."

"Enough with the suspense!" Mary said. "What's the problem?"

Bert swiveled his laptop around so the rest of us could see. I leaned forward to read the screen.

"We're wanted by the International Criminal Police Organization," he said. "Otherwise known as Interpol. As of now, we're fugitives."

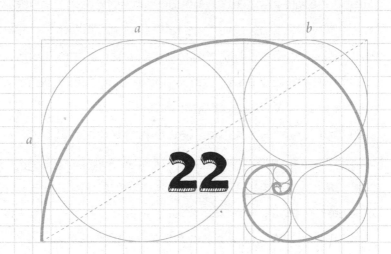

"And for the record," Bert continued. "The picture they chose of me is *horrible*. I look like a demented giraffe."

Mary rested her forehead to her hands. "How did this happen?"

Bert sighed. "It's got to be my height," he complained. "It doesn't photograph well."

"Not that," she said. She turned to Grace. "Wanted by Interpol? That's pretty huge, G."

"And we're kids," Charlie pointed out. "What the devil would make them actually think we're *that* bad? Isn't there some law about that? Because there *should* be."

Bert shrugged. "Looks like someone has been telling them we're part of a global crime syndicate," he said, turning his screen back to face him. "Pinning a bunch of diamond heists and bank robberies on us here in Europe. That's why the museum cops tailed us so quickly. They were already watching out for us. That stupid guard probably thought we were checking the place out before robbing them! We walked right into it."

"Don't forget the statue," Grace pointed out. "I bet he suspected we were behind the plaque vandalism, and were coming back to the scene of the crime to rub it in. Or steal something for real."

"Oh, codswallop. These *police*," Charlie squeaked. Her nose creased with disgust. "If we were going to steal diamonds or money or even some statue, there's no way we'd get caught. That would be counterproductive."

"Right?!" Grace said. She reached over Bert and grabbed his laptop. "Ugh, it's a bad picture of me, too. Why do they always pick the worst photos, where my face is all smirky?" She scrunched her face and mimicked the one in her photo.

"I'd steal the Statue of Liberty," Mo said, returning to his pasta. He swirled his fork in some sauce and slurped up the noodles loudly. "There'd be no place to put the thing," he added. "But I think it would be fun to try. What about you, Charlie?" He nudged her with his elbow.

Charlie smirked. "What would I steal? The Crown Jewels," she said thoughtfully. "And then I'd use the money I got for them to build the biggest, best wildlife preserve in the country. The Tower of London can't be *that* secure, right?"

"Wait," I interrupted. I couldn't believe what I was hearing. Not the stealing thing—I knew what *I'd* steal, too, if given the chance—but the fact they were so . . . so *normal* about all this made zero sense to me. This wasn't some wanted poster tacked on the bulletin board at a local YMCA. This was Interpol.

"You guys are acting like this happens all the time," I said. "A massive international investigative organization is after us. We're fugitives now. The minute any of them spots us, we'll be hauled off to jail. Or worse." Something else dawned on me. "This also means that our whole trip was a waste of . . ." I trailed off as my eye caught the screen of Bert's laptop again. Six names were listed as fugitives.

Six.

I couldn't hide the panic on my face. "Tesla, what is it?" Grace grabbed the laptop again, suspicious. It didn't take her long to notice what everyone missed. Very slowly, her mouth dropped open. She hoisted the laptop and turned it, sweeping the table so we could all see it. "Anyone see anything weird about this?"

Mary and Bert gasped in unison.

I clenched my jaw, darting a look to the exit before I could stop myself. "Guys, it's got to be an accident," I said.

"There're only six of us on the wanted list," Charlie said softly.

"Every one of us *except* Nikki," Bert said.

Six electrons, six kids wanted by the police. I couldn't make that math look good. But I knew as well as they did that there was only one reason I'd be left off the list—and it *wasn't* good.

"How is that possible?" I tried to play dumb, desperate for someone to jump in with an answer. "I've been with you the entire time. Anyone could identify me as easily as any of you."

"Except when you were at the police station," Mary said. Her tone was gentle, but she was starting to lean toward the others. Away from me.

"Did you tell them anything?" Grace asked. "About the academy? You didn't tell them our names or anything, did you? Or about Martha?"

My fingers squeezed the stem of my fork until my knuckles were white. There was no way I was going to let them think I had something to do with this. I hadn't betrayed them. I thought *they* had betrayed me.

"No!" I said. "I told them I was on a school trip. I even pretended *Finding Nemo* was my life story to fill the time. That's it, I swear!"

You know that feeling when you're telling the truth, but you *know* nobody believes you? So then you look extra guilty because of it and your eyes get all twitchy and you can't hold a normal expression? That's what was happening. They kept looking at me, waiting for me to say more, their eyebrows quirked and mouths pinched together.

"And you can't think of any reason why you'd be protected from this list?" Bert asked. His eyes narrowed ever so slightly, making me jerk back in my chair.

How to Look Guilty
by Nikki Tesla

Step 1: Sweat a lot.

Step 2: Avoid eye contact. Stare at your spaghetti instead.

Step 3: Fidget as much as possible.

Step 4: Make sure your voice gets all high and squeaky.

"*Protected*?" I asked. "How?"

Charlie bowed her head slightly while Bert and Mo exchanged glances. Only Mary and Grace would look me in the eye. I crossed my arms over my chest, desperate to counter the exposed feeling washing over me. What exactly was Bert saying?

That someone with a background in crime kept me off the list.

Did they think my father was the someone involved in this, just because he'd broken the law many times over? The question hit me like a charging bull. My mind flashed back to when I'd spoken to Martha on my first day at the academy. She'd promised me that nobody knew my family history. Nobody knew about my dad at all. But here they were, implying I had some sort of protection from the law.

I forced my face to be as neutral as possible, refusing to give into the scream in my throat. Mom and I had been running from what he'd done for years, but I couldn't even escape him on another continent. Would people always see me as a criminal? As someone who couldn't be trusted?

"Are you completely positive you didn't say anything to the police?" Grace asked again. "How else would they know who you were with? It's okay if you did. We . . . we have to know, Nikki. You said so yourself. You thought we abandoned you back there . . ."

"That's because I don't fit in with you, okay?" I blurted. Pickles, sensing the change in mood at our table, climbed onto my lap protectively.

Grace turned to Mary, who looked at me searchingly. "Is that why you told the police about us?" she asked quietly. A hush fell over the group, and that familiar, prickly feeling of awkward shame settled on me like a heavy mist.

I wanted to give her a good answer, but for once, I didn't have one. I had no idea how they'd ended up on a most wanted list. I also didn't know why *I* wasn't on it with them, which made everything feel much worse.

My voice hitched in my throat. "I mean it," I said. "I didn't tell anyone about you. They must have gotten your info from someone else. Someone framed you, but it wasn't me." I picked nervously at Pickles's fur. "I swear."

The team didn't say anything. An uncomfortable silence blanketed the table, which made the noises of the café around us even louder. I fought the urge to avoid all their stares. *This* was why they weren't my friends, after all. Why friends never worked. They might have saved me back at the station, but they did not trust me.

I fought to conjure my shield again. This time it would be completely impenetrable, made of an undiscovered element that keeps out every potential friend that might trick me. It would be big enough to protect me and designed to focus on the only things that mattered. *Find your death ray. Protect Mom.*

I kept my voice calm. I knew the truth. "Honestly," I repeated. "I didn't—"

"It's okay," Grace interrupted. She held her hands up, like she wanted to change the subject. "If Nikki says she didn't rat us out, then she didn't."

I should have been relieved to hear her say that, but I wasn't. Instead, a tight fist clenched around my heart, unwilling to let go. The group stared down at their plates, except for Mary, who inspected me quietly.

"I have a theory," Mary finally said.

I turned to her, grateful for the interruption. Hopefully her theory didn't involve me selling them out.

"Alexander Zarn," she said simply. "Whoever he is, he left us a clue to get us all here. It's possible *he* wanted to frame us."

That made a lot of sense to me. If only the rest of them would see it that way.

"But why?" Bert asked. "And why frame all of us except Nikki?"

The group was quiet for a moment. Nobody had any idea. Bad news for a table full of geniuses.

"Maybe he's wanted to frame us for ages, but this was his best opportunity? It would get us out of the way," Mary offered. "And Nikki's only been at the academy for a couple of days, so it's possible he didn't know to include her on the list."

"Darn right it's possible," I muttered, absently feeding Pickles a piece of my pizza crust.

Finally, Leo spoke up. He tapped a breadstick against the table. "If we can figure out what Zarn wants with the death ray, we'll be one step closer to understanding why he's targeting us."

Grace nodded. "You're right. We still have our plane and pilot. Mary, do you think this Zarn guy would expect us to go after him together?"

Mary took a deep breath before answering, tucking her hair behind her ear. "No," she said. "I think he was trying to split us up. To turn us against Nikki. He's expecting us to kick her out of the academy, and go back home so we can tell Martha about what happened in person. That's my guess, anyway."

I gulped and kept my eyes on my plate. Why would Zarn want to get me kicked out? How did he know the others would assume I'd rat them out? *Would* I have betrayed the academy if I'd been stuck in that police station any longer? I didn't know the answer to anything these days.

Grace stood up. "Good," she said. "If that's what he expects, then we do the opposite. We're not going home. We're going to him. Got his address, Leo?"

He swiped his phone. "An apartment complex in Zurich, Switzerland. About six hundred miles from here. Two hours if Marcus takes us."

"Let's go," Grace said. "The sooner we figure this guy out, the closer we are to that death ray."

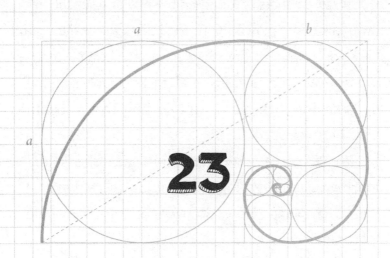

23

If you're keeping track, I'd already been stuffed into a sinking plastic cage and nearly drowned, sent to investigate a naked guy with the world on his shoulders, been captured and interrogated by Italian police, and eaten more pizza than I could shake a fork at. And now I was about to break into a high-rise apartment in Switzerland to track down information about the guy who supposedly stole my death ray in the first place.

It was turning into quite the Tuesday.

"All right." Grace held the binoculars to her eyes and peered through them, surveying a group of tall gray apartment buildings.

Spotless windows reflected the evening sunset, and a few apartments glowed with the blue light of their giant televisions, which were easy to spot mounted to their walls. It was hard to imagine all these people simply living their lives right now, with no idea that a madman could be so close to them.

"We've got a ritzy condominium," she said. "A doorman. Definitely high security in there. Let's hear your best plans. How do we get into Alexander's apartment?"

When we got to Zurich, we decided to plant ourselves on some park benches near Alexander's address and scope the place out. The good news was it was getting dark out, making it easy to disappear in the shadows. Judging by the layout of the building and the address Leo found, Alexander's home was on the fourteenth floor in a corner of the building. There were no lights on and the curtains were drawn shut. We had a perfect opportunity to get in there and find out what he was up to.

But first, we needed to break in.

"We could pretend we have some Girl Scout cookies to deliver to him," Mary said. "It's not the most technologically advanced idea, but everyone loves Thin Mints."

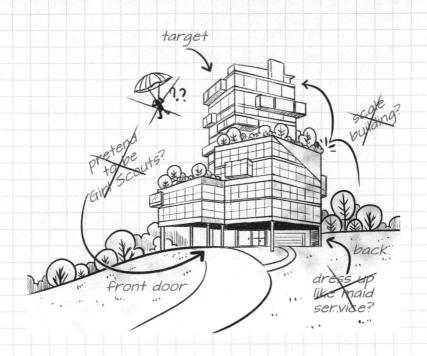

Mo shook his head. "I don't think they have Girl Scout cookies in Switzerland. And even if they do, the doorman will make us leave them at the door for Zarn to pick up. A doorman's whole job is to not let anyone up without tenant permission."

Grace nodded. "The doorman's a problem."

"What about canvassing to raise money for a charity? Oh!" Charlie pointed to a man walking a spotted Dalmatian on a leash. "Spreading the word about pet adoptions! We could borrow a dog and say we're raising money for the local dog rescue."

Grace chewed her lip. "That *could* work."

"Some apartments don't allow pets because of people with allergies," Mary said, shaking her head. "We're better off with something less . . . furry. What do you guys think?" She turned to Leo and Bert. Leo was busy scribbling something on his notepad, while Bert hunched over his laptop and ignored us.

"I got it," Bert said. He lifted his head and looked up through his hair.

"We're listening," Grace said.

"No," he said. "I mean, I got into the building's security system. We need to wait for the guard to go to the bathroom, then you can walk right in. You'll need to pick the lock on Alexander's door, but that's easy peasy."

Grace grinned. "Now we're talkin'. Who wants to do the dirty work? Tesla, you should go. You know the death ray, so you'll have the best chance of spotting something useful in there. Mary? How about you? Or Charlie?"

Charlie held up her hand. "I'll go," she said. "If we're caught, there's a chance I could buy us some time. Blonde hair."

I blinked at her, confused. "What difference does that make?"

"Alexander's got light blond hair, too. Charlie could pretend to be his long-lost daughter if you got caught," Leo said.

Charlie nodded, confirming his theory. "It could give us a few seconds to react if we're cornered. Any plan that gives us an edge is the right one," she said, tossing her blonde ponytail playfully.

"Let's get started," Grace said. "The doorman's been drinking coffee this whole time. He'll go on a bathroom break soon and you two can move." She pointed to Charlie and me. "The rest of us will be on lookout duty in case Alexander comes home or the doorman gets any bright ideas about leaving his post."

"One more thing," Bert said. "You need to move fast."

"Of course," I said. "A relaxed break-in would be too much to ask for."

"It's not that," he said. "When I know you're moving, I'll disable the security system for the building. That includes alarms, cameras. Everything. But once I do, the police will know it's happening. Based on the distance to the police station, you'll have eleven minutes to get in and out before they show up. Grace can probably buy us a few more minutes if necessary," he said.

Grace nodded. "I'll be watching, don't worry."

Charlie grabbed my hand like we were about to dance at a party instead of commit a felony. I handed Pickles over to Leo for safekeeping.

"Ready for your first home invasion?" Charlie said.

I glanced up to the fourteenth floor. Alexander's apartment was full of secrets. Full of answers. I needed to know what he was planning with my death ray.

I took a deep breath, preparing to lie. "I was born ready."

absolutely NOT ready!!!

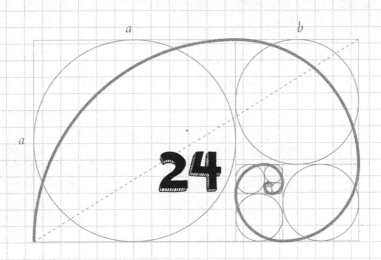

24

Coffee must really work quickly because it didn't take long for the doorman to disappear into the bathroom. Charlie and I creaked open the front door and bolted inside. The smell of warm, stale coffee flooded my nostrils. A coffeemaker, huge but nearly empty, sat on the front desk. Our doorman didn't simply *like* coffee. By the looks of the mugs scattered around his workspace, he was trying to hit a new caffeine record.

"We've got time," Charlie affirmed as we headed for the stairs. There was no way we'd risk getting caught red-handed in the elevator. Or worse, stuck in one, if Bert's security plan failed.

"Can't we think of a way to race around *without* turning into sweaty messes?" I panted. With eleven minutes to get in and out, we only had a moment to scale fourteen flights of stairs. My legs and butt were aching!

"Only three more flights!" Charlie said. "And don't worry—you get used to it!" She wiped her brow with the back of her hand and kept up her quick pace.

When we reached Alexander's door, I checked my watch. My heart was trying to out-run itself in my chest. "We only have seven and a half minutes left!" I sput-tered, wheezing to catch my breath. "More like five if we want to leave enough time to get out of here before the police arrive."

"Here, let me," she said, nudging me aside. She pulled a small leather case from her bag and whipped out a metal tool that looked like a cross between a screwdriver and a needle.

"I guess I should pay attention to Advanced Lock Picking when we get back," I said.

"It's easy. Even a toddler could manage it," Charlie said, not looking up from the lock. "This is your typical pin tumbler lock. You need to lift all the key and driver pins to the right height and then . . ." Her eyes closed and she listened intently for something.

Click.

"Righto," she said. She stuffed the case into her back pocket and gingerly tested the door. It opened without a sound. "After you?"

I braced myself and stepped inside. My eyes swept the area around the door, checking for booby traps of any kind, but the place was clear. Alexander hadn't been expecting us.

"Looks pretty normal," Charlie said, stepping forward into the dark. She turned on the flashlight on her phone and held it up.

The place was tidy, with slate-gray and black furniture lined up in straight, 90-degree angles. A kitchen decked out in stainless steel appliances sat to our left, and a living room area spanned the other side, flanked with floor-to-ceiling windows.

"You take the left side, I'll do the right," I instructed.

Charlie nodded and crept around like a mouse, moving quickly through the papers and envelopes on the kitchen counter. Every so often, the flash of her phone's camera flickered in the dark, as she took a photo of an address or name that could be useful.

I tiptoed through to the living room. Sofa. Television. Two glass coffee tables without a speck of dust on them. And then, along the far wall, an absolute flurry of papers, maps, and notes.

"Uh-oh," I said.

"Everything okay?" Charlie's voice was barely a whisper in the dark.

I swallowed and held up my phone to light the area.

Definitely not okay.

A huge wall-sized map of the world was pinned up, with hundreds of Post-it notes, newspaper articles, and seemingly random scribbles. I let my eyes drift from left to right, trying to make sense of it all. Words flashed before me, but so far, none of it made sense. Ellesmere Island. September 17. The date was circled several times in ink of different colors.

My hands began to tremble and I nearly dropped my phone to the floor.

September 17 was two days from now.

Then a single pin nearly gave me a heart attack. It

was stuck right into my city on the map, with a tiny note tucked under it. Written in small, neat handwriting was my full name and address. A bright red arrow had been drawn to the note, and it had been circled several times so hard, the pen had gone right through the paper to the wall on the other side. The words *SHE WILL HELP* were scrawled angrily beneath it.

She will help? Was he talking about me? He must be. Why on earth would he think I would help him with whatever he was planning? How had he even known who I was or how to find me? Was he only looking for my death ray? Or was Alexander looking for something more?

I reached out and unpinned the note. A small metal object fell to the floor, and I hopped back, terrified I'd set off a booby trap. Holding my breath, I realized with embarrassment that it was only a metal keychain clattering against the floorboards.

"What was that?" Charlie hissed in the darkness.

"It's fine," I said. I wrapped my hand in the bottom of my T-shirt to hide my fingerprints and picked up the keychain. "It's just a keychain . . ." I trailed off.

Staring at the keychain in my palm, my vision tunneled and my whole body stiffened. The design was two spiral coils, no bigger than an inch or so across with shiny, worn edges and dirt in between the markings. Jagged bolts of lightning shot from the toroid on top at odd angles. I recognized it immediately as a resonant transformer circuit, meant to produce high-voltage current. I had plenty of them back in my lab at home. They were kind of old fashioned, but I'd always thought there was something magical about the vintage-looking tech.

But it wasn't the spiral coil that nailed me in place. It was the faint scratches on the back of the keychain that did it. A tiny, messy *Nikki* that I had etched with a protractor from my geometry set.

This keychain belonged to my father.

They say time travel isn't possible, but in that moment I wasn't in Zurich, Switzerland, anymore. I was five years old, in our living room poking away at a pile of books while my parents argued. I don't remember much about my dad—he died not long after that argument. The spiral keychain was the last thing he picked up before he left for good. I can still hear the jingling of his keys as he snatched them from the porcelain dish by the doorway. He always told me the keychain was his lucky charm.

We'd all assumed his belongings had been destroyed in the laboratory during the blast that took his life. The one that was a trial for the bomb he was supposedly planning to set off a week later in a public place.

So it was true, then. Zarn not only knew about me and my death ray, he'd somehow known my father. Zarn could have even worked with him. How was I going to explain this to the others without telling them who I really was?

"Whoa!" Charlie said, scaring me back to reality and cutting off the millions of questions swirling around my head. She skittered around the sofa to get a better look at the wall. Before she made it, I pocketed the note and keychain without thinking.

I turned around red-faced. "Intense, right?" I said, trying to cover for myself. I don't know why I didn't want Charlie to see the note or Dad's keychain. It was obvious that Alexander had known about me. That was how he knew to follow me to Genius Academy and steal my death ray. But the part about him believing I would help him—and practically *counting* on it—felt way too incriminating. Everyone already had their doubts about me. With the keychain here to connect me to Dad's horrible history, I'd look even guiltier. I couldn't risk them being any more suspicious. Not before I found the death ray and made sure Mom would stay out of prison.

"There has to be a clue here," she said. Her camera phone flashed again as she took pictures of the whole area. "I wish we could take it all with us. Any guesses on what he's planning with the death ray? We have to leave in sixty seconds," she reminded me, flashing her phone.

I shook my head, embarrassed. I'd been so busy freaking out that I hadn't paid attention to the real reason we were here. My mind raced to take in the contents of the wall. "He's obsessed with magnetic poles," I said, pointing out the lines drawn from the northern and southern poles of the map, and the mathematical equations scribbled beside them. "He's also been following the stock markets for a long time."

She took a photo of the equations. "You, Leo, and Bert can take a look at the math when we're back," she said. She frowned, then spun around to where a black wooden desk sat, nearly empty. Compared to the messy wall, it looked like a museum exhibit. Only a few blank papers and a pencil sat on top.

"He's got to have a laptop nearby," she said, narrowing her eyes. She knelt on the floor and stuck her head under the desk. I heard a couple of thumps, followed by a creaking sound as Charlie shimmied out with her arms outstretched, easing out a piece of the desk.

"Secret compartment," I said, impressed. "How'd you know where to look?"

Charlie pulled a laptop from the drop-down compartment and winked at me. "Usually the smart ones leave things where people least expect them. Which is to say, where *we* most expect them." She tucked the laptop under her arm as the sound of whining sirens grew outside the window.

"Shoot!" she said.

My phone buzzed in my hand. A message from Grace flashed in all caps.

GET OUT OF THERE, BACK EXIT.

She didn't need to tell me twice.

"Grace says to go out the back," I said, dashing for the door with Charlie chasing after me. My fingers curled around the crumpled note in my pocket.

I still didn't know what Alexander was planning.

But no matter what his note said, I was not about to help him.

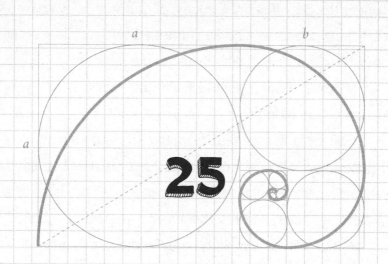

25

There is no better place in the world than the library. You can learn about anything. Go anywhere. Be anyone. And it's an especially great place to hide after breaking into someone's apartment.

Before Genius Academy, the library was where I'd spent most of my time, apart from the makeshift lab in my room. Hidden behind books, it was easy to lose myself in other worlds, and meet people who went on huge adventures.

I never thought I'd meet people like that in real life.

And I definitely never thought I'd be one of them.

I was dragging my feet a few yards behind Charlie when the library's automatic door whooshed open for us. We had plans to meet everyone in the youth room, so when we walked in, we grabbed a few random books from the shelves to make it look like we were meeting for a study group. Charlie sashayed her way across the room, but Alexander's laptop was locked under her arm in a viselike grip.

The room was lined with beanbag chairs, tables, and tons of books. Sinking down into a purple beanbag, I did my best impression of a kid worried about an upcoming math test. I haven't ever actually *been* worried about one, but I imagined it was a lot like worrying that your death ray had fallen into the wrong hands. Imminent doom, fiery death, panic, and all that.

"Close call?" Mary asked. She tossed two chocolate bars at Charlie and me. "Eat up. It will help with nerves."

"Too close," Charlie said. She tore into the candy with her teeth, but I tucked mine in my pocket next to the keychain. Despite not having eaten in hours, my appetite had vanished. I made sure to keep my eyes down, especially around Mary. Could she sense how freaked out I was? That psychic brain of hers was probably picking up all sorts of guilty signals. I distracted myself by holding an arm out for Pickles, who was still happily perched on Leo's shoulder. Ever since losing her in Italy, I hated the feeling of being without her for too long.

"But that's why God invented emergency exits," Charlie continued. She was eating so fast, she had to gulp for air between bites. A smear of chocolate stained her bottom lip. "There was a huge world map on the wall with all sorts of equations and notes. Something about magnetic poles ... investing companies. Banks. Here." She passed Zarn's laptop to Leo. He opened it gingerly, like he was expecting it to blow up. After a few keystrokes, he nodded.

"It's going to take a while, but we can get into it," he said.

"Did you notice anything useful, Tesla?" Grace asked. "Anything at all that can give us some hint to what he's planning?"

Yeah. He's planning on getting me to help him. And because he knew my dad, we can pretty much bet he's a first-class bad guy.

I couldn't say the words out loud, but they were practically screaming inside my head. What would *I* think if the situation were reversed? If Grace or one of the others had found such an incriminating note?

I knew darn well I wouldn't trust her. Especially if she was new to the academy, like me. I didn't have a choice here—there was only one solution that made sense. I had to sort this out before telling them. But knowing that didn't make it easy.

"I'll have to look over the pictures on my phone," I said, focusing on a sliver of truth. "There's probably something in those equations, but I'll need a few minutes to go through them. Who are the math lovers here?"

Mo, Leo, and Bert raised their hands.

"Grace, you should take a look, too," I said. The image of the world map flashed in my head again. "I've got a bad feeling about this." That part was true, at least.

"Sounds like a plan," Grace said. Before she could continue, a symphony of buzzes rang through the room. Grace's and Leo's phones, receiving a message in unison.

Leo was first to read it. "Crud," he said.

I braced myself. I was beginning to notice the only time Martha texted us was when she had bad news.

But this time, it was Marcus. Our pilot. Leo read the text, his face solemn:

Major problem. Delayed by police. Plane going to be seized. Can't fly you home. Don't text, phone compromised.

Grace set her jaw. "This is a hiccup."

We all exchanged looks, and I wondered if everyone else was feeling the same anxious, walls-closing-in-around-them feeling that I was. Without a plane, we were completely stranded here. How long would Marcus be detained for? Now that the rest of the team were fugitives, there was no way we could even get near a commercial flight to get home. For a brief moment, I considered taking off without them and trying to find Zarn myself. But without their resources and Martha's help, I knew I wouldn't make it far on my own.

I was trapped.

Grace set her phone down and closed her eyes. A small wrinkle appeared between her eyes, and she rubbed her temples with her fingertips. For a second, I thought her usual tough-as-nails exoskeleton was going to crack.

I should have known better.

"Our to-do list right now," she said calmly. "Techies, get into that laptop. Math nerds, see if you can crack those equations and figure out what Zarn is planning with that death ray. We head home and do what we can to find him. Nothing's changed."

"Wait," I said. "Everything has changed! What are we going to do if we actually find him? We don't even have a plane to get anywhere." Pickles seemed to agree with me. She rushed over to Grace and began nipping gently at the bottom hem of her pant leg. If Grace minded the nuisance at her feet, she didn't show it.

"We *do* have a plane," Grace said. Her eyes leveled on Leo, who had finished off his chocolate bar and was licking his fingertips. "Now we need a pilot."

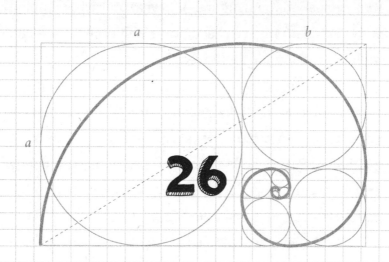

26

Grace used a fistful of foreign bills to get two taxis for us to the airport.

"For emergencies only," she'd said. I wasn't sure if Martha would agree that our plan constituted emergency conditions, but last time I'd checked, Martha was still cozy at the academy mansion without international police forces after her, so I wasn't sure she got a say in this one.

The seven of us lined up outside the chain link fence facing the runways. To anyone else, we probably looked like a bunch of bored kids watching the planes take off. Nobody would suspect we were about to hijack a four-ton private jet.

"You're sure you want to *steal* our plane to get home?" I asked. Trucks and those weird stair cars drove around the tarmac every few minutes, ferrying luggage and boxes to their destinations. There were people—security, travelers, and airport employees—everywhere I looked. And lots of people meant lots of eyeballs to witness everything we did.

"I think it's a great idea," Charlie said. "I mean, it's not even really stealing if you think about it."

"That's right," Grace said. "It's our plane. At least, it's the academy's plane. *We're* the academy. We're taking it home because it's the right thing to do." She stood tall as she spoke, but there was definitely a hint of uncertainty in her eyes.

"Downside," Bert interrupted. "People aren't usually happy about kids stealing planes, whether or not they own them. Which we do."

"Come on!" Grace said. "Remember when we broke into the Federal Reserve last year? This will be *much* easier! Think about it. It's only a jet. Leo, you took those helicopter lessons once. Flying a plane can't be that different. Plus you've built a few."

Leo didn't look convinced either. "Those weren't exactly planes. More like primitive flying machines. I suppose the physics are the same, but there's still the issue of actually getting us on board without anyone noticing." He turned to me. "I don't suppose you've invented a teleporter yet, have you?"

I grimaced. "No, but it's on my list."

"We can't leave the academy jet here," Grace said, throwing her arms in the air, like "here" was a desolate wasteland, rather than the gorgeous Swiss countryside. As far as retirement homes for our plane went, this one was pretty swanky. "Martha would lose her mind. We're practically doing everyone a *favor.*" She scanned the airfield with her hands on her hips. "What do you think, Charlie?"

"The best way to stop someone from noticing something is to make them focus on something else," Charlie said. She used her hand to shield her eyes from the sun and watched the airport workers intently.

"Misdirection," Grace said.

"Exactly," Charlie said. "Explosions. Loud noises. Big events. The pope."

"We pull anything like that and they would shut down the whole airport," Mary said. "That kind of distraction would work against us."

"Right," Grace said.

"What about a *good* distraction?" Mo asked. "Can that ferret of yours do any tricks that would draw a huge crowd? How about dancing or fire eating?"

I made a face. "She can fire a death ray," I muttered. "Isn't that right, Pickles?" I turned my head to nuzzle her as she perched on my shoulder. "*That* seemed to draw our neighbors' attention . . ."

Mo didn't get my inside joke, so I tried again. "We need a sign that says 'Free Pizza.'" Outside in the fresh air, my appetite was returning and my stomach rumbled at the thought of cheesy dough. Our earlier carb-fest in the Italian café felt like it had happened weeks ago.

Grace's eyebrows knit together in concentration. "Hmm . . ."

"I was only kidding—" I started to say. But she held up her hand.

"Brilliant," she said.

"You can't be serious," I said. "I hardly think that free pizza will get anyone excited."

"No," Grace said. "But tempting people with a good distraction will. A diversion. What if, say, a famous celebrity stopped by today? Somewhere at this airport well away from our jet? Everyone would flock there, I bet."

Mary's face lit up. "Ooh! That could work. If Prince Harry were here, that would definitely be a good distraction." She fanned her face dramatically and swooned.

"Definitely dreamy," Mo said. "But how do we get him here?"

"Come on," Leo said. "You guys are supposed to be smart. We don't need *him* here. Though I know you'd be totally cool with that, *Mary*." He scoffed, rolling his eyes.

She beamed and fluttered her lashes at him. "Darn right."

He continued. "We just need everyone to *think* he's here. And how do we do that? Where does everyone get their celebrity news these days?"

"The Internet," I said, finally cluing into his plan.

Leo took off his backpack and set it on the ground, making a spot for himself on the grass. Squinting up at us against the sun, he opened his laptop. "All I need to do is take over a celebrity buzz website and post that Prince Harry will be here at . . ." He checked his watch. "How's half an hour for everyone?"

"Works for me," Grace said.

A few keystrokes later, Mary and Mo began scouring social media on their phones to see if Leo's plan was taking off.

"It's working," Mary said. "Twenty-two thousand people are tweeting right now." She read aloud. "Prince Harry and Meghan's clandestine visit to Switzerland is said to be taking place in the next hour."

Mo finished the article, reading the rest aloud in a faux high-pitched British accent. "Royal watchers, don't miss your chance to spot this royal cutie. *Hashtag* Prince Harry Vacay!" He raised his eyebrows at the screen. "Look, there's a picture and everything. He *is* dreamy."

Grace took his phone and scrolled through some of the posts. "Thank you, gossip mill!"

● princelyupdates84.
Harry is here!

● MarryMeHarry99.
what!! where?? ♥ ⮂

● royalwatcher.
omg! gate? ♥ ⮂

● windsorluv:
BRB flying to
Switzerland
♥ ⮂

★

"For the record? That's a terrible English accent," Charlie quipped.

Leo stood up and brushed a few blades of grass from his pants. "That celebrity website is going to notice pretty quickly that I posted a fake article for them. When they do, they're bound to shut the rumor down."

"Look!" Grace said. "The airfield is already beginning to clear." She pointed to our jet. It was the smallest aircraft on the tarmac, but since it was our only way home, I couldn't wait to hop on board again.

"No time like the present," Charlie said, tugging her bag higher onto her shoulders. "Off we go."

Mary trudged alongside me, peeking over her shoulder toward the building. Was it me, or were her feet dragging a little?

"You know he's not really there, right?" I said, unable to hide my grin.

She sighed dramatically and picked up the pace. "I was hoping the power of suggestion would work on him," she said bitterly. A small smile quirked her lips. "Can't blame a girl for dreaming."

Grace's voice drifted back to us, half-giggling. "Gonna need more than a dream to get this plane off the ground! Move it!"

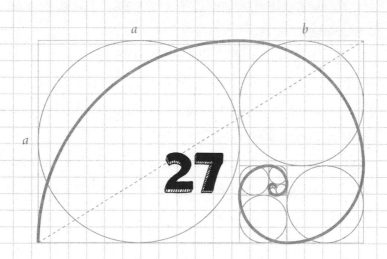

The sun burned hot in the sky as we rushed toward our jet, staying in a tight, straight line. Leo's fake Prince Harry post was working, and behind the glass of the airport windows, clustered silhouettes rushed toward the arrivals area of the airport. Everyone wanted a glimpse of the superstar royal. It was scary how quickly the word got out on social media.

"Hurry up," Bert said, leading us to the plane in long strides. "We'll only have a few seconds before we need to enter the code. Forty-five seconds! *Go!*"

We hiked up the steps to the jet two at a time, and dumped our backpacks in the seats. Bert punched a security code into a small panel on the wall. The faint mechanical sound of the stairs lifting told us they were folding up into the plane. For a moment, we were completely silent. The air inside the plane was hot and stale, like an oven that had been turned off minutes earlier.

"Is that it?" I said, fanning myself. The jet appeared much bigger than it had on the way to Italy. Outside the window, the tarmac was still empty. Any minute now the crowds would realize they'd been fooled and that they were as likely to see Prince Charming as they were Prince Harry in that airport.

Leo grabbed me by the hand, catching me off guard. I'd never held hands with a boy before, and the fact it was happening for the first time as I stole a plane made butterflies, *no*, giant eagles, wing around like crazy inside my stomach. How could something make you feel excited *and* terrified at the same time like that? It didn't make sense.

I dropped his hand and kept marching ahead. *Don't lose focus, Nikki.*

"We're not quite done," he said, leading me toward the cockpit. "Now we need to actually fly this thing."

I followed him through the cockpit door. "What makes you think I can help you fly?" I croaked.

He plunked down in the captain's seat and put on the set of headphones by his side. "You're an inventor. You get this stuff. The others have their strengths, but you and I have the best chances to get this plane home. Wanna be my copilot? It'll be *fu-u-un*." He gestured to the chair beside him.

My stomach flip-flopped again as I peeked around the space, unable to stop a smile from creeping onto my face. My palms began to sweat. From the plane? Or Leo? Both were giving me a mild heart attack, but the realization that we needed to get this thing off the ground scared the you-know-what out of me. The cockpit contained two seats side by side and dozens of controls. It looked a little scary, but after a few minutes of inspection, I started to read some sense in all the black and gray switches and knobs.

"Is there a manual?" I asked. "This must be fairly simple."

"Yeah," he said. "Get enough lift to stay off the ground and then we'll be flying." He winked at me. He passed me a headset, which I tucked over my ears. I sat down in the cocaptain's seat and gave myself a mental pep talk.

No big deal. Just a transatlantic flight. People do it all the time.

Not people. *Pilots.*

Which I definitely was not.

Eek.

"Do you have an eidetic memory?" Leo asked.

I nodded, and he handed me a manual from his side of the cockpit. "Take a look," he said. "Might find something useful in here."

I reached up to touch each of the controls and gauges, familiarizing myself. Airspeed indicator. Artificial horizon. Turn coordinator. Heading indicator. Altimeter. Vertical-speed indicator. In front of both of us was the flight control column. I'd seen enough "bad guys take over the plane" movies to know that was the control that acted as a steering wheel that gave us lift.

"Are you two ready to go?" Grace popped her head into the cockpit. "Getting kind of antsy back here. We don't have much longer before we're noticed!"

"Nikki's finishing up with the manual," Leo said. "Then we'll be taking off."

Grace rolled her eyes, but her teeth bared in a perky smile. "You guys are such nerds."

"Takes one to know one," Leo quipped. "Tell everyone to buckle up."

Speeding through the manual, I checked and rechecked the flight instruments in front of me, making sure I was reading everything correctly. I tried to steady my breathing by counting to five, in and out, in and out. Understanding the theory was basically the same thing as doing it for real, right?

I could *do* this.

"Don't worry," Leo said. "These things practically fly themselves."

I kept my eyes forward, certain that Leo would pick up on my anxiety if I gave him a chance. "I guess we'll find out, won't we?" I flipped the manual closed. "How are we on fuel?" I began going through the steps of take-off as fast as I could.

Leo tapped the gauge. "Full tank."

"We're supposed to get permission to take off," I said. "From air traffic control. Or else they could shoot us down."

Leo made a face. "Houston, we are requesting clearance to be awesome," he said without turning on his radio. "We're in Switzerland," he continued, tapping the fuel gauge again. "No way they'll shoot down a small jet like this. Next up is flaps." He adjusted the control to 10 degrees, like the book suggested. Despite his arguments, it was obvious he was pretty comfortable flying this thing.

"Now we push the fuel mixture knob. Advance the throttle," I said. Hearing the plane whir loudly around us made the intricate system of engine and gears in my head come to life. I swallowed down my fear as Leo followed my instructions, pushing the red knob slowly, and we began to move. There was no doubt that people outside would hear us. What if someone ran over? Or tried to stop us by getting in our path on the runway? I'd read somewhere that birds were a risk for planes. What if there were *birds*? What was the goose situation in Switzerland?

I squeezed my arms in tight against my chest and hoped for the best. If Mary could hope against all odds that Prince Harry would really show up, I could hope for this to turn out safely. The whirring of the engine—even louder now—began to shake my entire body.

"Everyone hang on!" Leo shouted over the noise.

My breath caught in my throat as we gained speed on the runway. Outside the cockpit window, the runway sped by beneath us and the trees on the horizon came closer and closer. Everything was a blur.

"Don't hit the trees," I muttered. "*Don't* hit the trees."

The nose of the plane began to lift ever so slightly, and I knew that was our cue.

I grabbed the control column and pulled back gently. The sound of rumbling wheels on pavement below disappeared, and the path became smooth and much quieter. We were airborne!

Oh God.

We were *airborne*.

Leo let out a long, shaky breath, darting a look out both sides of the cockpit window. "*Ooo-kay* . . . We've got this." His voice was barely audible.

With a shaky hand, I steadied the column and kept lifting us higher, keeping an eye on the vertical-speed indicator. I opened my mouth and worked my jaw, letting my ears pop. The sounds around me became muffled. It didn't take long to reach cruising altitude, and the plane purred like a large mechanical cat under my fingertips. We'd made it.

"Nice one!" Leo said finally, reaching up for a high five. "We keep her pointed west and don't bump into anything, and we're practically home already."

I gripped the column tightly and nodded once, trying to convince my heart to start beating again. I'd done it! Part of me wanted to jump for joy. But the other part felt completely in over my head. With the jet, the weird zinginess still coursing up my arm after holding Leo's hand, and my complicated feelings about the keychain in my pocket, I almost wanted to grab a parachute and take my chances with a free fall.

I closed my eyes for a moment. But I wasn't envisioning my shield like usual. This time, I was imagining my room at home. Pickles. My books. My lab. *Mom.* This was all to keep her safe. I opened my eyes, resolve firming up inside me. *Find your death ray.*

"You okay?" Leo asked. "You're looking a bit pale." I dodged out of the way as his hand reached to touch my forehead. My heart couldn't take any more zings at the moment, no matter how floppy and cute his hair was when it fell into his eyes.

"I'm good!" I yelped.

Way to be normal, Tesla.

"Your hands say otherwise," Leo said, nodding to my lap. I'd been tapping my fingertips nervously on my pant leg without realizing it.

"Just a little Morse code," I choked out, eager to come up with an excuse for my jitters. I cleared my throat and sat up straighter. "All pilots are required to know it."

He lifted his eyebrows. "Is that so? Well then, I guess we're both qualified." He reached over to the flight column and tapped out a sequence of dots and dashes. My heart raced as I stitched together the letters into words.

Nice flying, Tesla.

"Thanks," I said. I knew from the heat in my face that I was blushing something fierce. I tapped out a response.

You too, cocaptain.

Those giant eagles were back. I held my breath to keep myself from saying something embarrassing out loud.

If he noticed I was acting more bizarre than usual, he didn't let on. "I'm setting the cruising engine speed," he said. "We're on our way home, but it's going to take a while." His eyes narrowed and he tapped the compass control on the dash. "Hey, that's weird."

"What's wrong?" I leaned forward to inspect it. The needle was whirling around, fighting to find north. Leo sighed loudly with relief as it righted itself, pointing in the right direction.

"Huh," he said. "Must have been a glitch."

I let my shoulders relax, grateful that we weren't stuck on a jet with faulty equipment. But something about the image of the faulty compass stuck in my mind as I stared forward at the blue horizon. Ice-white clouds speckled the sky. We couldn't have asked for a better day for flying.

"Tesla!" Grace's voice rang out from the cabin, distracting me from the clouds. "You might want to get in here. Bert found something on Zarn's laptop."

I jerked my head around to look out the door at the team, worry pawing at me like a kitten with a string. Did Zarn have information about me on his laptop? How much did he know about me because of my father? I stared out the window for a moment, wishing I could speak to Zarn myself. I wanted to chew him out for even trying to involve me in whatever he was planning.

"Go ahead," Leo said. He gestured to the window. "I'll keep an eye on things."

"Thanks," I said. I pushed up out of the leather seat and headed to the cabin, preparing for the worst.

Unfortunately, that's exactly what I got.

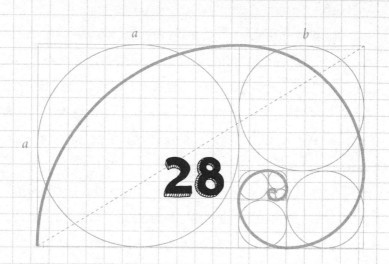

28

My hand reached instinctively for the keychain in my pocket before sitting down across from Grace. Mo, Bert, Charlie, and Mary each had laptops in front of them. Scattered notes and scrunched pieces of paper littered the floor around them. The cabin looked more like it belonged in a messy library study than a private jet.

"Bert got into Zarn's laptop," Grace said. "What do you make of this?"

My teeth clenched together as she handed me the computer and moved to the cream leather seat to my left. Skipping through the windows, I frowned. Many of the images were similar to those I'd seen on the wall of Zarn's apartment, including a world map with lines for the magnetic poles drawn on with neat hash marks.

Another window revealed Zarn's bank information, and a third showed his inbox, displaying his most recent emails.

I breathed out a sigh before I could stop myself. There was no mention of my name, my father, or anything that would make the team think I was working with Zarn.

"You look relieved," Grace said. She exchanged glances with Mary. "What are you thinking?"

I shook my head as if to clear it. "It's just a headache from takeoff," I lied. I started to click through Zarn's latest emails. There was nothing special about them, only a few online purchases. "He bought a parka last week," I mused.

Bert stood and leaned over the back of my chair, pointing out another email. "This one," he said. I couldn't help but notice that when *his* arm touched my shoulder, I didn't feel any zings. None at all. Apparently zings were dependent on the boy who gave them to you.

"We found these coordinates: 86.5°N, 172.6°W. I tracked them but they lead to the Arctic Ocean, smack-dab in the middle of the water. He'd need a parka there, but there's no land at all to stand on," Bert said.

I narrowed my eyes, jumping back into Zarn's apartment. Something—one of the notes on his wall—was poking at my attention. Finally, it hit me. "Ellesmere Island," I said. "Zarn had a note about Ellesmere Island, along with the date September 17. Those coordinates are to water, but they're close to the island. I bet he's headed there!"

Grace shook her head, frustrated. "We need to know what we're walking into. Is there anything about Ellesmere that could relate to your death ray?"

I considered this. Ellesmere Island was the northernmost part of Canada. But I had no connection to it, and I knew that my death ray didn't either. I didn't remember my dad ever mentioning the Arctic. Why would someone take a death ray to the tundra?

"Nothing's coming to mind, sorry." I scrolled back to the map of the earth. I sighed in annoyance. I was glad there was no obvious connection in his laptop, but with no clear hints to go on, we were sunk. What was Zarn up to? I stared at the map, trying to read between the lines of his plan. "The map in his apartment was the same," I said. "Remember, Charlie?"

"That's right," she said. "Those lines spread around each side of the world like two big donuts. I remember that, because it made me want a donut."

"They're magnetic lines. They start up at the North Pole and—" I stopped short. The compass in the cockpit bubbled up in my mind again. Whirring and twirling, desperate to lock onto true north.

"Hey." Grace nudged me. "You all right, Tesla? Need a water or something—"

I shushed her without meaning to, and squeezed my eyes shut, trying to piece it all together. Something snagged in my head, like a fish on a line, wriggling hard and frantic. I tried to concentrate, reeling the line in. *What was Zarn's plan?* The compass was important . . .

My death ray. Magnetic poles. Ellesmere Island. I pulled the line closer.

"Ellesmere Island is near the site of magnetic north," I said. "Isn't it? Can someone check that?"

I held my breath as Mo's fingers sped over his keyboard, but I already knew I was right.

"The coordinates," he said, nodding fiercely. "Those coordinates are magnetic north! And Ellesmere Island is a plot of land close enough to them to reach by plane."

"I know what Zarn is planning with my death ray," I said.

Guilt washed over me, followed by a dread so sharp and dizzying, I had to grip the arm of my seat. I couldn't speak. Why had I made that stupid thing in the first place? Because I wanted to? Because the technology alone made the horrible thing worth it? I'd been trying to create something that could help the world, but in the wrong hands, I'd known it could be a disaster. I didn't want to say it out loud, but whatever happened from this moment on—I knew—was all my fault.

In Zarn's hands, my technology could destroy the planet.

"Crikey," Charlie said. Her blue eyes were wide—she knew exactly what I was thinking. "He stole a bunch of magnets, remember? He's going to use them to amplify the death ray. And he's going to do it on Ellesmere Island. Isn't he, Nikki?!"

Grace blinked. "Spell it out for me, Tesla. We're not all inventors here. What on earth is going on?"

The sound of Leo stepping out from the cockpit made us all jump. His face was solemn, and I could tell by his expression he'd heard every word we'd said. I cowered forward, holding my head in my hands.

"What Nikki doesn't want to say is: Zarn has the death ray. He's on Ellesmere Island, which is the home to magnetic north of the planet. And he's going to use the death ray to switch it."

Grace's mouth dropped open. "Switch *what*?!"

"The magnetic poles of the planet," I said. Saying it out loud should have helped—you can't solve an equation without knowing the components of it—but this puzzle was more horrifying than I ever could have imagined.

Mary gasped. "Does that mean what I think it does?"

"On its own, my death ray is a dangerous weapon, but it can only target one person at a time," I said.

Bert nodded. "Right. The particle beam is focused enough for one location, but it's fairly small?"

"Exactly," I said. "But if you applied lots of electro-magnets to the design, that would focus the beams even more. It could heat up atoms at an incredible rate and . . ." I didn't want to finish that sentence.

"And then it would be a weapon that could do a lot more damage," Mo said quietly. "He really could do it. Zarn could switch the magnetic poles of the earth. He'll have the tundra to himself without any witnesses, too. It's the only reason he'd bring the ray to Ellesmere Island."

"Oh!" Charlie interrupted. "Atlas! That statue was holding the globe. Did that security guard say how the plaque had been vandalized?"

Grace frowned. "Yeah. He said that someone had swapped the Arctic and Antarctic Circles on the little map." She threw her notebook to her feet. "It was practi-cally spelled out for us, and we missed it!"

I ran through every option in my head, but it was the only thing that made any sense. Alexander Zarn didn't want to steal anything from the museum. He already had my death ray and the electromagnets. Why visit some museum in Italy and send us there to retrace his steps? There was only one logical solution: He wanted us to follow him to Italy and find Atlas. And that led to another conclusion.

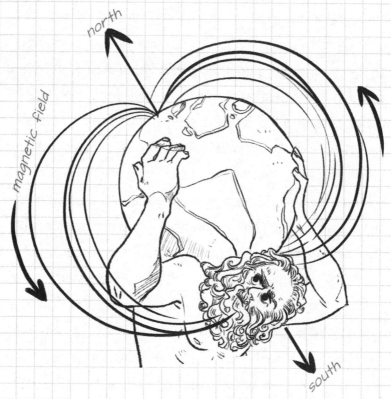

He wanted us to know *why* he wanted the death ray.

And he wanted us—or maybe even *me*—to know what he was planning.

But why would he wait for me to join the academy to take it? Wouldn't it have been easier to steal it from my house? I absentmindedly reached for my pocket again, feeling the outline of the note and keychain through my jeans. He wanted my help with his plan; I knew that for certain. Maybe waiting for me to join the academy was the only way he could see that I'd have the resources to come and find him? But how did he know Mom had called them for help? And was I playing into his hands by following him? What choice did I have? Theories raced through my head, threatening to crush me.

"I'm afraid to ask," Grace said. "For the non—geographical geniuses in the room. What *exactly* does reversing the poles change?"

I looked at Leo, remembering again our chaotic compass. Spinning out of control. Wild and lost. What if it never found north again?

"Everything," I said. "It changes everything."

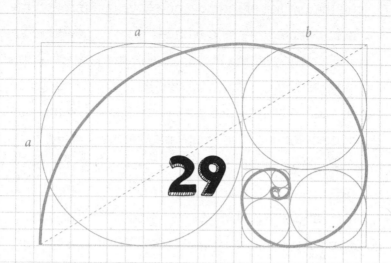

29

One of the great things about having a good memory is being able to remember all sorts of stuff you've read in books when you need it. One of the bad parts is there's no chance you can kid yourself. If something awful is about to happen, you know pretty much every detail.

My mouth felt cottony and dry. "There's a lot of iron in the earth's core, so it's basically like one giant magnet. The last time the earth's poles switched was seven hundred eighty thousand years ago. Usually, it takes place over the course of hundreds to thousands of years, so the results are slow. But it still has an effect on everyone."

Leo picked up for me. "With electromagnets to help amplify the death ray, Zarn could aim it near magnetic north, and mess with the magnetic field enough to completely switch polarizations. In other words, make north south and south north. Part of what protects us from the sun is the earth's magnetic field, so messing with it could make us susceptible to all kinds of solar flares. That can cause radiation, cancer … all kinds of health problems. It would be a global catastrophe."

"This doesn't sound right," Grace said. She rubbed her temples. "Steal your death ray to switch magnetic poles? It's so *random*. All so he could cause cancers? What kind of a supervillain is this weirdo?"

I stared down at my hands, unwilling to look her in the eye. The connection between my father and Zarn made guilt swim through me like a hungry piranha.

"We need to know *why*," Mary interjected. "What does he stand to gain by doing this? What's motivating him? Villains *always* have something motivating them, no matter how strange they act."

"Unless they're bananas," Mo muttered under his breath.

"Bananas is an option," Grace said. "But this guy is too logical. Too strategic for that. Stealing Nikki's death ray. Leaving us that clue."

Leaving a note saying I would help him, I thought ruefully.

I stood up and stuck my hand in my pocket, clutching the damp note. I should tell them about what I'd found. What I'd hidden from them. Maybe it would help us defeat Zarn. Could I risk it? My mind whirred at the options.

If I did tell them and they believed that I wasn't involved with Zarn, we could work together to find him and stop him. It's always best to have *all* the information, right? But what if they didn't believe me? If I were really trustworthy, I would have shown them the note when I saw it. I wouldn't have hid it from them in the first place. Only *guilty* people hide things.

That was a fact.

I also couldn't think of a way to tell them about the keychain without opening up about my dad and *his* history. Who knew if they'd ever speak to me again after they learned about what he'd done. With Zarn so obviously connected to him, they'd judge me based on my father's actions just like everyone else did.

I let that route play out in my head. If they didn't believe me, we'd waste precious time arguing. The team already suspected me of selling them out to the police. They would contact Martha for sure. She would tell them to keep me contained until they knew more. Best-case scenario, they would try to stop Zarn without my help. They wouldn't risk trusting me. I wouldn't if I were in their shoes. I already didn't fit in with them, and that would verify their suspicions.

That was the *best* outcome. But the worst-case scenario? Zarn would use my death ray to switch the poles, and Genius Academy would kick me out forever. Global catastrophe should have been the scariest possibility in my mind, but the truth was, the most terrifying thing of all was something much simpler.

Mom.

I had to work with the others to stop Zarn because it was the only way to keep Mom out of jeopardy. *After* we stopped him, they would never need to know about the note I stole, or who my dad was. They would trust me, I wouldn't be kicked out of the academy, and Mom would get to stay right where she was, safe in our house. She wouldn't get locked up because of *me*, or something I'd done. And even if the others ever *did* find out about my father, they'd know I wasn't anything like him because I'd already helped them defeat Zarn.

I swallowed down my guilt and left the note in my pocket. It was the only choice I could make that didn't end with me locked up until further notice.

Of course, nobody had noticed my indecision. They were too busy actually trying to fix the situation.

Bert furiously clicked the laptop keys. His mouth was twisted into a determined frown. "There's got to be something useful on here. Let me see."

"If the poles reverse, there are going to be massive electrical problems," Charlie offered. "It's likely that electrical grids will go right bonkers all over the world.

There'll be citywide blackouts. Chaos. Maybe Zarn's planning to exploit the pandemonium?"

"Can I see the pictures on your phone again?" Mary asked. She took the phone from Charlie and began swiping through the images of Zarn's apartment. "A person's home is a reflection of their mind-set," she said. "There's nothing here that makes me think he's out to cause mayhem. He's chosen neat, orderly lines. Fine art. This is a man who likes nice things. Very clean." She swiped through more of the images. Her eyes narrowed and she looked up at me questioningly. "Bad men usually don't choose to do evil things because they're evil. They pick them because they *think* it will bring them some kind of happiness. Do you think he's after money?"

I scoffed. "He lives in one of the richest places in Europe. I'm sure he's already got money."

Mary considered this, twisting the ends of her ponytail with her fingers. "True. But what's one thing that's better than a lot of money?"

"*Mo'* money," Mo said, pointing at himself.

"Whoa, hold up," Bert said. "We were wrong. Zarn *isn't* rich." Bert looked up at us, triumphant. "He *used* to be. But according to his bank records, he's not anymore. He lost three *million* dollars last year. It literally disappeared from his account, and he hasn't put anything new in since."

"I wonder how he lost it?" Grace said. "Gambling?"

"Can you see his investments? Check for anything that relates to electricity." I said.

Bert had the answer almost instantly. "Nothing."

"Wait a minute," Mary said. "We're forgetting something here. Leo, what did you say Zarn did for a living before he embarked on a life of crime?"

I thought back to the first time I'd heard Zarn's name, when Leo's handwriting analysis tagged him.

"Cybersecurity for a bank," Leo and I said in unison.

Grace sighed loudly. "So it *is* money!" she said, throwing up her hands. "He's going to fry the earth's magnetic pole, mess up all the electrical grids, and use his cybersecurity network to steal

his customers' money when the systems are down."

I nodded. "That makes sense to me." I drew in a long, slow breath as the full picture grew in my mind. Stealing money was one thing—that would hurt the people involved—but if Zarn planned on messing with the earth's magnetic field to do it, the whole *world* would be in trouble.

All because of me.

The only reason I'd even agreed to join Genius Academy was to keep Mom safe. And now she was at risk, along with the seven billion other people on earth.

"Leo," I said, snapping myself into action. I'd had enough thinking. It was time for action. "Think we can reroute our course?"

"To Ellesmere Island?" he asked.

I nodded. My voice was small in my throat. "We— *I*—have to stop this guy."

Grace lifted her hand. "Now, hold up." She glanced at Mary for a beat and grimaced. "We can't forget the original note we found at the academy. It's possible *all* of this is a plan to get us to follow him there, like we did to find Atlas. If we proceed, we need to have each other's backs, okay? The whole thing could be a trap. *Again.* Last time we did what he wanted, six of us ended up on an international wanted list."

I pressed my lips together. The idea had crossed my mind. Zarn's note was practically *proof* that he wanted me on Ellesmere Island. Especially since he'd known my father. And here I was rushing off after him. Was I leading us all into a trap? There were too many unknown variables in this equation. The only way to determine what those variables were was to make a move.

"I have to go after him," I said. "If you guys don't want to, I understand. But this whole thing is happening because of my death ray. I need to make sure Zarn doesn't use it."

And I need to protect Mom by cleaning up this mess.

"We're a team," Grace said. "All for one and one for all, and all that. We go to Ellesmere Island and stop this maniac. Everyone in?"

The team nodded and lifted their fists to the air. "To the Canadian tundra!" Leo said. "Home of polar bears, melting sea ice, and magnetic north!"

After our decision, I helped Leo with the plane's course correction and settled into the copilot's seat to watch over things while he took a nap. As I watched the shifting clouds drift by beneath us, a pang of homesickness rang through me like a deep, low bell, resonating through every cell. What would Mom say if she could see me right now?

The answer to that, I knew.

It was a simple equation. First, she'd tell me I was absolutely nuts to make the death ray in the first place. But then she'd tell me to do whatever I could to stop someone from using it to ruin the world.

I wouldn't let her down.

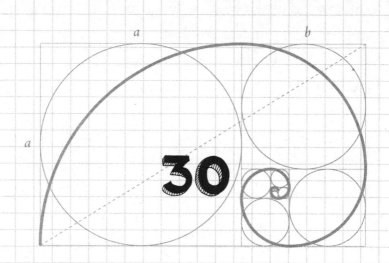

30

A couple of hours later, Leo tapped me on the shoulder and offered to take over the controls so I could sleep. I went back to the warm cabin, nestled down in the comfy seats, and closed my eyes, but our plane was almost to Ellesmere Island, and the sound of the engines kept me awake.

Well, that's kind of a lie.

It was really the impending doom. But whirring engines sounds much more poetic.

Hauling myself from my chair, I tiptoed around the others. They were fast asleep, with their heads lolled to the sides. I made myself some of Charlie's tea in the tiny galley kitchen and wrapped a blanket around my shoulders.

Returning to my seat, I noticed a pair of shining eyes staring at me through the dim light of the cabin.

"Can't sleep?" Mary whispered. She climbed up from her seat, dislodging Pickles, who'd been napping with her, and sat down beside me. Pickles scampered after her and crawled back into her lap.

"Not really," I said. I peered at the others to make sure they were still out. I sighed, letting my shoulders sink. It was nice to have a few moments of quiet. "Starting an apocalypse sort of messes with your head." I wished I could tell her about everything else that was weighing on me, but I couldn't risk it. No matter how understanding she appeared, her allegiance was to the others, not me.

"It's not your fault, you know," she said. "The whole thing with the death ray, I mean. You couldn't have known someone would steal it or, or that they would try to use it in this way. We've all gotten into sticky situations like this. It happens when you belong to Genius Academy." She stroked Pickles's fur absently. I could tell my ferret trusted Mary. Pickles didn't let just anyone get this close. Especially if they didn't have a pocket full of French fries.

"Have *you* ever been the cause of a global catastrophe before?" I asked, nestling farther into my seat.

Mary shrugged. "Charlie was once caught in a plot to assassinate the British prime minster. A total misunderstanding, of course. Albert *accidentally* released radioactive isotopes into a shopping mall in Oregon." She leaned in closer. "You should have seen Martha after that one. If looks could kill!"

I giggled. "Really?!" It was hard to picture any of the team getting into trouble like that.

Mary tugged her blanket higher to her chin. "Yep. We've all been there. But we always figure it out in the end."

A dull ache returned over my heart. That was yet another reason I wouldn't fit in with them. They might create problems like I did, but I definitely didn't have their knack for solving them.

For a moment, the only sounds in the cabin were the gentle whir of the plane's circulating air and Mo's rhythmic snoring. Knowing almost everyone was sleeping made it a little easier to let bits of the truth out.

"I really didn't rat you guys out to the police back in Italy," I blurted. "I know the Interpol wanted list makes me look really bad. But I swear I didn't."

"Oh, I know that." She waved her hand. "You had no reason to."

"You really can read minds, can't you?" I said, half joking. I wouldn't be surprised if Mary was the smartest out of all of us. With those quick-darting eyes that missed nothing, she was certainly the cleverest.

"I wish," she said. "I can usually see where someone is headed. And I can tell when people are lying. I think it's because to tell good stories, you really have to know your characters. And to write good characters, you need to know people really well. I knew you were a cool person when we first met you back at the pool."

My mind drifted to that first day at the pool. How I'd treated everybody. "I was a jerk to all of you," I said. "I didn't want any of this to happen."

The beginnings of tears pricked at my eyes, but I blinked them away. The stress was starting to unravel me. Zarn. Mom. Death rays. Hidden notes. Even the ghost of my father hung over me like a shadow. I wanted to come clean, but my shield was impossible to crack open.

"I was homeschooled for a while," I admitted. "And before that, everyone I knew at school thought I was a giant weirdo. Mom had to take me out. I've never really had . . . friends."

I breathed a little easier, saying some of the truth out loud. After news of my father's death—and what caused it—everyone at school thought I would turn into him. Especially since, like him, I spent all my time in a lab. I could still remember their whispers and nervous glares in the school hallway.

"It was the same for most of us," she said. "Albert, Leo, especially Mo. For two years, Mo didn't even talk. He only played instruments. Kids in their schools thought they were practically aliens. Charlie spent most of her time hanging out with her pets, so people never really got to know her either. Bert got shut in his locker so many times before he came to Genius Academy that he *still* has a phobia about combination locks!"

I giggled. "What about Grace?"

"Grace is different. She got recruited to Genius Academy *because* she was so good with people. Everyone wants to be her friend. And if you haven't noticed, she's very good getting out of tight spots! The point is, you might not have fit in with anyone at your old school, but with us, you've got friends. We could use an inventor here."

"Talk about a plot twist," I muttered.

"You can say that again," she replied. "Just know that no matter what happens, we've got your back."

I scoffed. "Even if I mess things up even more and Zarn wins and the whole globe gets turned into a magnet gone wild?"

Mary glanced at the others, who were still sleeping. "It won't happen. You're too smart. Zarn is another greedy old fool. We can deal with that."

"I hope you're right," I said.

The overhead lights began to flicker on, first sporadically, then all at once until they were all beaming down on us. Then a static-filled voice chimed in over the audio system.

"Attention, passengers," Leo said. "This is your captain speaking. Please bring your seats into their upright positions. We will be landing at Ellesmere Island in approximately ten minutes. I repeat, we are landing in ten minutes."

The cabin stayed silent for a few moments. Mary's eyes flicked up to the speaker above us. "He likes you, you know," she said. Her lips tipped up into a tiny smile.

"Who?" I blinked at her. *"Leo?"* My insides began to jitter, betraying my thoughts.

"Yep," she said. "I can tell. Do you like him, *too*?" She was teasing me now, shimmying her shoulders in a little dance.

"What? No!" I said.

"Good," she said. "That's what I told him."

I gaped at her and jerked my head to see if the others were listening, but they were still shifting under their blankets, slowly waking up. How could Mary say that to Leo? I didn't *not* like him. I mean, of course I liked him. But did I *like* like him? How could I even know? Just because someone gives you zings when they hold your hand and giant eagles in your stomach when they smile at you . . . does that mean you like them? He was definitely the cutest guy I'd ever met who also knew about death ray technology. But did that mean anything? Even if I did like him, which I'm not saying I do, why would she have done that?

"You told him I didn't like him?!" I sputtered. Heat crept up my neck, spilling into my cheeks. It suddenly felt like it was a hundred degrees in here. "Why would you say that?!"

Mary grinned. "That reaction tells me you might, after all." She winked at me. "Don't worry. Your secret's safe with me."

"Hey, you *tricked* me!" Some genius I was turning out to be. I didn't like what she'd done, and now that she'd put a magnifying glass on my jittery feelings for Leo, I was more exposed than ever, as though she could see every thought in my head. Exposed, but also . . . *giggly*? This was almost more confusing than a global meltdown. Argh.

Mary yawned, clearly unfazed. She stretched her arms over her head and handed a still-snoring Pickles over to me, then leaned down to touch her toes. "Sorry," she said, giving me a sweet smile. "Sometimes we don't know how we really feel until someone gives us a little shove into finding out. You're *welcome*. He'll never want to let Marcus fly this jet again, by the way." She gestured back to the speaker. "He's having way too much fun with this."

I hid my embarrassment behind my hands for a moment, pretending to rub my eyes as Grace and the others slowly began to wake up. I watched them stretch and roll their necks to get rid of the kinks from sleeping upright. Mary patted me on the shoulder in mock sympathy.

"Hey, guys." Leo's voice over the sound system made me jump. "What do you call a pilot who lives danger-ously?" There was a brief crackle and then Leo spoke again. "HAN YOLO!" His laughter filled the cabin as everyone rolled their eyes, buckled their seat belts, and prepared for landing.

"We're up, we're up," Grace muttered. She glared at the intercom, as though Leo could see her from where he sat in the cockpit.

Grateful that the moment with Mary had passed and nobody had heard my conversation with her, I went to help Leo land the plane. Mary might have used her Jedi mind tricks to zero in on some of the confusion in my head about Leo, but there was no way I was going to let it show on my face. I kept my gaze forward as I plunked down into the cocaptain's seat.

The view nearly took my breath away. Mountains, valleys, rocky terrain, and crystal sparkling lakes spanned in front of us like a postcard or a magical land that had never been touched by humankind.

"I've got us set to touch down right at the closest land position to magnetic north," Leo said. There was a note of warning in his voice. He pointed directly ahead of us, where a small hut was built on the otherwise pristine landscape.

"That's either Zarn or we're about to encounter some really unlucky ice fisherman," he said. A dark grimace crossed over his face. "When we land, we won't have long to sort it out."

Sort it out.

Right.

That was a funny way of saying, *get back my death ray before the world is ruined.*

"Okay," I said. I gripped the flight column as we descended, squinting against the early morning light. "Let's save the world, shall we?"

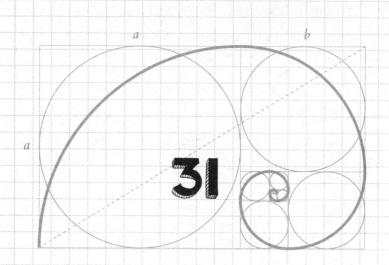

Here's the thing about saving the world: It never goes the way you plan it.

Our jet landed smoothly on the snow-spackled ground. Promising her extra treats if—no, *when*—I returned, I secured Pickles away from harm in my backpack and locked her in the cockpit, terrified to lose her in this feral terrain.

The seven of us piled out of the plane, grouping in a semicircle to watch one another's backs. The hut sat in front of us, looking as innocent as a fishing station or hunter's refuge, with a thin plume of smoke trailing from the chimney.

For a moment, I worried that we'd miscalculated, and we really were about to give some poor old ice fisherman a heart attack. But my pulse started knocking hard when I peered around the side of the hut. The death ray—my death ray—sat on a man-made tripod aimed directly at the ground. Three rows of electromagnets were duct-taped along the tripod's legs. By the look of the snow, the death ray hadn't been fired yet, but Zarn hadn't wasted any time getting it into position.

My mouth went bone-dry.

Before I could make a run to grab it, the rickety door of the hut creaked open. Out stepped a thin man, with icy-blue eyes and skin as white as the snow around us, stretched over his bony face. He looked exactly like the picture that Leo had found, but with a shaggy scruff of white-blond beard now masking his cheeks.

"Zarn," I said. I sounded like a cheesy character in a movie. But what else do you say to the guy who'd sent you on a worldwide wild-goose chase? Already, my veins were buzzing with adrenaline, my breath short. There was no mistaking his plan now. This guy was planning on ending the world, all so he could steal money from the unsuspecting masses.

But I was not expecting the next words from his mouth.

"My dear Nikola!" he said, greeting me like an old friend. He rubbed his gloved hands together and started toward us. His big boots clomped in the snow, spraying white dust in the air. "I've been expecting you! I'm so glad you made it. I take it you received my note!" His voice was light, with a hint of an eastern European accent.

The team held their ground, but there was an unmistakable shift in the air at his words. Grace darted a look at me. "Tesla, what's he talking about?"

I shook my head, unwilling to let him throw me off. "Nothing, Grace. He's trying to mess with us." I had to lie.

Zarn shuffled closer to us, letting his gaze drift over each of us in turn. I flinched away when he got to me.

"So this is Genius Academy? The world's best and brightest!" He bobbed his head up and down like he was inspecting a new car, and not quite pleased with what he saw. "Not much to look at, are you? Just a bunch of kids. I was hoping Nikki would learn some important lessons from her time with you."

"Back off, dude," Mo said. He edged to the front of the pack, his large frame blocking us from Zarn's cold assessment.

Zarn looked past him, examining Charlie, then moving to Grace and Mary. "Which one of you is Ms. O'Malley?" he asked. "Your fearless leader? That would be . . ." His finger twirled in the air pointing between Mary and Grace.

"Right here, jerkwad," Grace said, unmoving. "Now, how about you hand over that death ray you stole, before the police arrest you. We're here to give you a chance to surrender peacefully."

My breath choked out of me, in a frozen cloud. Was Grace bluffing him? There was no cavalry coming. Even if Martha knew we'd need the help—which she didn't—it would take hours for anyone to get here. But the quick twitch in Zarn's eyelid told me he wasn't sure what to believe. I forced my head high, pretending I was as confident as Grace. This was her specialty, getting what she needed. I had to trust her.

"Well, if that's true then I'm afraid our time is short!" He pointed to me. "Nikola! Come with me, and you can enjoy the final stage of this grand plan of mine. Maybe it will entice you to make some new weaponry for me. There's lots of money to be had, you know. I work for some lovely people who are *very* excited to meet you."

People. That meant there were others in on this. Leo and Bert exchanged glances, clearly thinking the same thing.

A sharp bark of a laugh erupted from my throat. "Money? Are you kidding me? I'm not helping you with anything. We're here for the weapon—my weapon— and then you're going to jail."

Zarn's eyes locked onto mine, and a slow smile grew on his face like a crawling, poisonous vine. "So you *haven't* told them, have you?"

I tried to play dumb while the others shifted on their feet. I could feel their stares, niggling at me from all direc- tions. "There's nothing to tell them," I said.

Keeping my eyes on Zarn was the only way I could say the words out loud. The lie was too big for me to hold on to anymore. Bigger than the unending landscape of snow around us, and even colder.

He clicked his tongue. "And what if they already know, hmm?" He turned to Grace. "For a group that's supposed to be *all for one*"—he lifted his hands and waved them around dramatically—"there sure is a lot of lying going on! But I know something you don't."

"And what's that?" Leo said, stepping forward.

Zarn's eyes twinkled and his face melted into a sleazy smile. "Now, I'm not s'posed to tell you any of this, y'hear?" His European accent was gone, replaced with a thick southern lilt. My thoughts raced to fish out where I'd heard that familiar drawl before.

A large man with eyes shielded by dark sunglasses swam out of my memory. One of the suits that had come to my house to discuss the death ray. The reason I had gone to Genius Academy in the first place. My breath hitched sharply as I pieced the puzzle together.

No.

"You're the agent who recruited me to the academy," I said, unwilling to believe the truth. How had I missed that? The man in front of me, tall but thin, bore no resemblance to the man who'd spoken to me that day at my house. Or did he? He was just as tall, but there was no trace of the giant muscles that had nearly burst through his suit that day.

A painful lump in my throat grew. He'd tipped his sunglasses at me in the kitchen, revealing his icy-blue eyes. The same eyes that stared happily back at me now. Such a sharp blue, they'd be recognizable to anyone.

Except for me, apparently.

It was all a cheap trick, and I'd fallen for it.

He bared his teeth at me in a devilish grin. "I'll admit, that disguise wasn't my best. A bodysuit and some nicely tailored clothes. But you were so eager to keep your mother out of trouble, you'd have looked past anything."

"What's going on, Tesla?" Grace's voice was low.

Fear wound itself up my chest, tightening its grip on my shoulders. I was running out of time.

"They have my computer, Nikola." Zarn's tone had changed again. This time he matter-of-factly ignored the others and spoke directly to me. "I left it for you in my apartment, of course! And I know your friends got into my emails. And I also know by the looks on their scared little faces right now that they read the journal entry I wrote about how important *you* were to my little plan! That you would meet me here, and that no matter *what*, you would understand why we should be working together. With your technology, my know-how, and my employers, we could make a *lot* of money."

His voice dropped dangerously and he spoke plainly. "They know about your father. And they don't trust you for a second, Nikola."

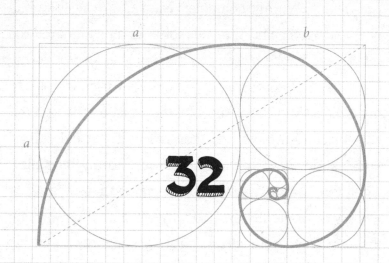

32

My heart fell. He'd planted some bogus journal entry as evidence to make me look guilty? And they believed it? How could they? But then, that wasn't any worse than what I had done, lying to them to avoid their judgments. It's funny how you can think you're doing the right thing at the time, but the minute it comes back to bite you, you can see how amazingly stupid it was. I was no genius. I was the world's biggest fool.

"Grace, it's not true. Whatever you read, it isn't," I said in a panic. I searched her eyes for any indication that she believed me. They were hard and unblinking, barely looking away from Zarn. "Leo, you believe me right?" I needed someone, *anyone* on my side.

He didn't answer, but there was a mask of sympathy

on his face. A sad smile. Like I'd let him down. Like he was saying good-bye. It was true. They thought I was just like my father, willing to destroy people's lives with this awful man.

But then why had they come all this way with me?

"I know you took the keychain from my wall," he said. "Your *father's* keychain, that is. That's why I left it for you, so you'd know I was on your side. Remember my note? 'She will help.' Why do you think I wrote that? I *knew* you had it in you to take your work to its full potential. Your father would be proud of you today, you know. You're set to become the world's greatest inventor. He'd want nothing more! I told him years ago I'd watch over you, and when the time was right, I'd help you find your rightful place in the world." The wind whipped the sound of his gleeful cackle, swirling it around us, and nipped at our ears. "You're much brighter than he ever was, Nikola. Your inventions will succeed where his failed. That's why you didn't tell these 'friends' of yours who you really are. Because you know deep down . . . you're not one of them."

All eyes darted to me, and my hand instinctively went to my pocket, as though I could block the keychain from view. I looked guilty. *Incredibly* guilty. And I knew it.

"How could you do it, Nikki?" Bert asked. "We wanted to trust you. To give you a chance."

I was shaking now, but not from the cold. "I didn't tell you about my dad or the note because I *wanted* you to trust me!" I said, desperate. "I knew you wouldn't believe me after you landed on that Interpol list. If I'd told you everything, I would have risked being kicked out! I *couldn't* let him win! I couldn't let my mom down either! Not *again*!"

The words came crashing out of me without any brakes. All my excuses had sounded so clear, so logical in my head before. But now? Teasing apart my guilt and fear was too complicated with Zarn staring me down so smugly.

"There's no way I'll help you," I said to Zarn. My throat was raw and scratchy. "You're crazy, but even you have to know that!"

"Don't you get it?!" I turned to Grace, desperate for her help. I needed her on my side before the others would join. "Look, I know what you're thinking. But he's trying to mess with us from all sides! He made me afraid to trust you, and planted evidence so you wouldn't trust me! All so he could split us up, so I would help him."

Zarn waggled his finger at me and shuffled toward the death ray. "Doubt is a funny thing, my dear. It creeps inside the best of us and feeds on every tiny white lie. But the good news is, everything went according to plan. These resourceful little prodigies brought you here to me. That's all that matters. Don't you see? That's why I wanted you to go to the academy in the first place." He looked with disgust at the others. "Not to join some *team* of geniuses. You needed to learn one final lesson. You'd never have agreed to join me until you learned that no matter what you do, you will *never* escape who you really are. No one will ever trust you."

Shame continued to crash over me. I knew he was right, but there was still no way I was helping him with his demented plans.

He kept pacing as he lectured, stopping only to glare at Grace haughtily. "I admit, I was a bit concerned when the police got ahold of you, but you championed through. And despite your cries of innocence, you're going to put all of your inventions to good use—*my* use."

"And why's that?" Clearly this guy was out of his mind, but there was something bone-chillingly creepy about how certain he was.

I followed him to the death ray, knowing I had only seconds before Grace and the rest of the team would rush me. I couldn't blame them for not trusting me. Zarn was right about that.

"Because you're very easy to read, that's why." He gingerly lifted the death ray from its tripod and passed it back and forth between his hands. Now that I was closer, I was able to get a good look at it. The barrel was clean, so it hadn't been fired, but the trigger was clicked into position to shoot. So much had happened since I first tried it out at home, and the smell of singed hair and wooden floorboards tickled my memory.

"I've known your father since before you were born, Nikola. I've also followed your accomplishments. You've never been one for friends. Bullied for your brilliance from such a young age," he said, giving me a sympathetic nod. "You could never trust others not to hurt you—to make fun of you—all for simply being brilliant. But *science.*" He clicked his tongue and gestured dramatically. "Science has always been there for you. Your inventions have never let you down. These people don't want to be your friends, Nikola. You know that in your heart."

He waved the death ray wildly, causing everyone to duck out of the way. "They want to *use* you. To shackle you up in some academy where they can keep an eye on you. But you know as well as I do . . ." His voice slowed, as though he was counting out the seconds before speaking again. *Two, three, four* . . . "Your curiosity is what makes you special."

I scanned the ground for anything I could use to get my death ray away from Zarn. A rope. A chain. Even a rock. But I knew he would shoot as soon as any of us moved. I was running out of time.

"You've got to be a little curious right now," he said sweetly. "What would happen if your little invention was used . . . on a human?"

He leveled the death ray at Grace's head.

"Zarn!" Leo barked. "Don't even think about it!"

Grace held her head high. Her eyes were fierce, and for once, I wished she wasn't so confident. I wished she would cower and beg—anything to get him to stop. Maybe he would let the team go if I promised to stay behind.

Mo, Charlie, and Bert edged dangerously close to Grace. But my feet were bolted to the ground, unwilling to move to save her.

"Go ahead," Grace spat, her arms outstretched at her sides like she was flying. She was challenging him.

"You know what?" Zarn said. He lifted his hand to the sky with a dramatic flourish. "I think I know what will convince you to really set your curiosity free." He turned to Mary. "You. You're Mary Shelley, correct?" His voice was high-pitched now. "The academy's resident writer? The character genius extraordinaire?"

Mary sneered at him, but didn't flinch as he beckoned her closer.

"What's the best way to get someone to do something?" he asked playfully. "You know, to *really* put their heart into it?"

Mary pressed her lips together tightly. Shaking her head slowly, she said, "I'm not playing this game with you. You aren't going to win."

Zarn erupted in a loud buzzer sound. "Wrong! *Motivation!* You know that better than anyone, don't you? Why do your characters do seemingly awful things? Motivation—a small squeeze—is all it takes."

Snow crunched under his heavy boots as he made his way to the front of the cabin, keeping the death ray lifted high in case any of us followed him. He reached out to crack the door open.

"Time to motivate our little Nikola," he said. His smile dropped as he shoved the door farther open and reached inside. "Come on out!" His voice echoed across the icy landscape.

The door creaked. He grabbed a blindfolded woman, and gripped her tightly to his side. The scream I'd been about to let loose died in my throat.

"Join us, Ms. Tesla," Zarn said. My mother, who had been haunting my thoughts since I left home. Who I'd wanted to protect more than anything. All my lies and desperate attempts to stay at Genius Academy boiled down to her. Every equation in my head disintegrated. She was all that was left.

The blindfold around her eyes was knotted tightly and her hands were bound. She took small and careful steps, feeling around with her feet to avoid falling.

"Mom!" I was frantic, taking her in from top to bottom. She wasn't injured from what I could tell. At the sound of my voice, she jerked her head in my direction, clawing desperately at the ropes around her wrists.

Zarn swiveled the death ray and pointed it at my head, forcing me to stay in place.

He hadn't gagged my mom, so the panic and fear in her voice were crystal clear. "Nikki! Nikki, are you okay?! I'm right here, Nikki!" The sound daggered through me. She was trying to console *me.*

"I'm right here, Mom!" I cried. "It's going to be all right!"

But it wasn't. None of this was all right. It was the definition of all *wrong.*

"Now, this is what I like to call motivation," Zarn said. He grabbed hold of my mother by the shoulder and dragged her a few steps closer to Grace. "You want to see how this weapon works, Nikola? I'm going to need you to prove to me you want to work together. You have my word, *billions* of dollars will be yours. Along with all the lab space you could ever dream of . . ."

Grace set her jaw. Mary and the others darted uncertain looks back and forth. Their feet were planted and their hands were held at the ready, but they didn't dare move. They had no options left either. Being a genius didn't matter when someone you loved was at stake.

I knew what was coming, but that didn't stop the tremor of madness from rippling through me when he spoke next.

"Choose," he said. Zarn was gleeful, practically giddy. He'd been waiting for this moment. "Your newfound *friend*?" The word dripped with poison. "Or your mother."

Nobody moved.

I eyed the death ray again, then caught Grace's eye.

"It's okay," she mouthed at me. Her eyes were soft, and there was no trace of anger in them. She turned her head ever so slightly to address the others and a shudder of emotion and admiration ran through me. Even with a gun to her head, she was being our leader. "It's got to go this way. I get it."

A thousand moments flashed back at me. The team's openness when we first met at the academy. Grace patting me on the back after saving me from the police station in Italy. Mary joking with me about Leo. Even Leo himself, sent to the academy at five years old, swam in my mind, swirling with the kids at my old school, viciously bullying me. All my desperate attempts to make a single friend that had failed. Mom's disappointed face every time we had to move to a new town because of who we were. How had I not seen these were all variables in the *same* equation? Mom. Genius Academy. My shield.

Nikki doesn't fit in with others.

The equation finally made sense. The shield that I'd conjured around myself didn't protect me at all. All it did was keep me from trying, keep me from finding or discovering anything or anyone new. Hadn't I learned that on this trip? I was an *inventor*—I shouldn't be letting one equation rule my life. I should be calculating, building, creating my way through tough situations, finding the people that really mattered to me. And here, on this frigid tundra, I'd found them. Grace was willing to die to protect me. They'd all shown up for me, even after reading those horrible things on Zarn's laptop. Even after discovering that I was the daughter of a madman.

Every one of them had found a home at the academy. They didn't fit in anywhere else, but they did fit with each other.

Zarn had known my biggest weakness. My shield was only hurting me, and it was why Mom—*everyone*— was at stake now.

I'd figured it out.

But I'd made the discovery too late. A chilled whisper of wind in my ear tickled me back to reality. The thick lump in my throat was going to choke me. I knew what I had to do, but I needed help. Maybe Grace had the right idea. All my life, people worried I would turn into my father. That I'd become a mad scientist, threatening the whole world. And maybe they were right after all.

I had to stop running. There was only one move left for me to play. To use the madness to my advantage. To own it instead of hiding from it.

I had to let the madness out.

"Grace," I said to Zarn, refusing to cower any longer. If I could truly fit in with the academy, now was the time to find out.

"I can't let you kill my mother," I continued. "Shoot Grace."

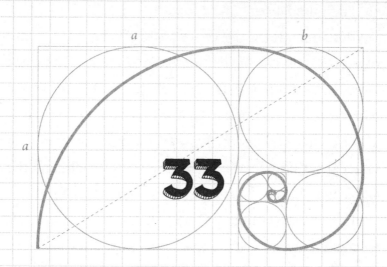

33

As if on cue, the team erupted in protest and stormed toward us.

"Tesla!" Bert said, leaping. He tried to grab me by the shoulder, but Leo got to him first. He held Bert back physically, but couldn't keep Bert's rage-filled words from hurtling at me. "How could you?!" Bert struggled against Leo's grip on his shoulder.

"Not so fast, gentlemen," Zarn warned. He retreated slightly, keeping the death ray pointed at Grace's chest. My mother shuddered, her head whipping back and forth. Despite her blindfold, she was trying to get her bearings. The group grew still, but their faces twisted in sneers and grimaces. I knew the team was certain they were about to watch their leader die.

Zarn's finger rested on the trigger. For a moment, he said nothing. Then his cheeks lifted in a slow, sinister smile, embracing the moment. "My dear *Nikola*!" he raved. "That is more like it! I knew you had it in you! Are you seeing the truth, now?"

"Nikki!" Leo hissed. "What are you doing?! We need to work together here—you *can't* do this! Don't give him what he wants!"

"Sorry, Leo," I said. "I know you thought I was going to be one of you. To be part of the academy." I spoke so fast, my words slurred together in a muddled panic. I slammed my hands against my thigh to make my point. My fingers tapped wildly as I spoke, desperate for Leo to listen. "But Zarn's right—I've never had friends. And I never will. Science is all that matters. You heard him. Billions of dollars is a lot of money." I turned to face Zarn. "Do it. I'll help you. But you're going to give every *cent* of any money we make to my mom, okay?"

Mary stepped forward. Her face was hard, determined. "Nikki," she said softly. "*Stop this.* There are other ways to end this."

I turned to face her, staring her down. "Sorry. Sometimes life throws you a plot twist."

Mary's eyes flicked to Zarn, and her feet shifted beneath her. Grace squared her shoulders, but turned her head to face me in her final moments. Her brown eyes glistened with tears, but she refused to blink.

"Enough. You've made your decision. Let's see how much death is built into this invention of yours," Zarn said, shifting the aim from Grace's chest to her head. "Good-bye, Grace."

The wind whipped up into a frenzy as Zarn pulled the trigger.

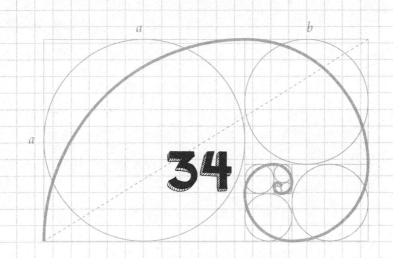

34

What happened next was unexpected.

That is, unexpected by everyone *except* me. That's the thing about being an inventor. You know things about your inventions that nobody else does.

Grace didn't get vaporized. In fact, when Zarn pulled the trigger, nothing happened except an unsatisfying *click*. He wiped his runny nose with his sleeve, and tried again, giving the death ray a good shake before aiming it at Grace again, and firing.

Ready for the moment, Mary leaped into action. She dove at Grace with her arms outstretched, while Mo and Bert followed behind, shielding her from Zarn's vision. The four of them fell to the ground in a pile of winter parkas and flailing limbs, while Leo reached down and scooped a handful of icy shards and snow in his palm and whipped it hard at Zarn's face. Zarn exploded in anger. He batted at his eyes furiously as Leo stayed low as he rushed him, tackling him and tugging the death ray from his hands. Then Leo grabbed my mother and shoved her out of harm's way.

"Leo! Give it here!" I held out my hand.

His cheeks were flushed, but he handed me the death ray without question. "I almost missed it," he said, panting. Beads of sweat sparkled above his eyebrow, turning quickly to frosty drops in the cold. "That was the fastest Morse code I've ever seen." He stalked over to help the others. Now that the death ray was in my hands and Zarn was restrained by five members of the team, Zarn stopped struggling.

"I was terrified you'd be too busy listening to what I was saying to pay attention to my hands!" I said, heaving a sigh of relief. I helped Mom to her feet and pulled off the blindfold. Her eyes watered like crazy in the bright Arctic sun, but once I'd used Mary's penknife to cut through the binds on her wrists, she was quick to hug me.

"Nikki," she breathed in my hair, hugging me tight.

"Nikki, are you okay? I can't believe you did that! I thought that poor girl was going to die! How did you *get* here?!" She wiped her eyes and gripped my hands.

"It's a long story, Mom," I said. I hugged her again, but made sure not to let Zarn out of my sight. "I'm okay. Grace will be fine, too."

Mary and Mo tugged Zarn to his feet. They'd tied his arms behind him, and he was spewing curses left and right. Bits of frozen spittle stuck to his face like disgusting leftovers from a past lunch. I stepped in between him and Mom.

"You've made a huge mistake here, Nikola," he said. "You could have had so much! I expected so much better from you! First a shoddy invention, and then protection for people who are only using you!"

Mo gave him a shake. "Enough, loser," he said. "It's over."

"Excuse me?" I said. I aimed the death ray at Zarn's left eyeball. "Did you say my invention was *shoddy*?"

A fraction of Zarn's usual theatrics returned, and he curled his lip in disgust. "Ms. Tesla," he said. He looked down at me from his long nose as he squirmed. "You've proven to me that your death ray does *not* work. You can't use it to threaten me now."

I flicked a tiny green switch that I'd added to the death ray's handle.

"Wrong," I said.

I twisted on the spot, aiming the death ray at Zarn's hut and pulled the trigger. A hot white bolt streamed forward, bathing the hut in brilliant light before blasting it apart like it had been hit by lightning. There were no remnants of wood left behind to litter the ground.

Zarn's face went pale.

"For someone so smart, you should have done your research," I said. I flicked the safety on again. "I have a ferret, you know," I continued. "Her name is Pickles. I nearly died testing this thing because I didn't have a safety on the trigger. Did you know that?" I aimed the death ray at his face and clicked the trigger, making him flinch. "Like I said. *Research*. Next time, don't mess with geniuses."

You can't blame me for *one* awesome movie one-liner, can you? I mean, I had him right there! And he was practically peeing in his snow pants!

"What do we do with him?" Charlie asked.

We all looked to Grace. So far, she'd been silent, but it was clear by the way her eyes flicked to my death ray that the idea of using it on Zarn wasn't out of the question. She shook her head, frowning.

Mom made it clear. "You are *not* to murder that man, Nikola Angelina Tesla," she warned. "He belongs in police custody and then prison for life." She wrapped one arm protectively around my shoulder, and the other around Mary.

Grace nodded. "Your mom's right. You saw the warrants out for his arrest," she said, smiling sweetly. "I vote we take him back home with us, tied up, of course. I'm sure the police will be happy to deal with him."

"Done," Leo said. He and Bert began dragging Zarn to the plane, while the rest of us followed behind.

"And Tesla? *Nikki*," Grace said. She wrapped her arm around my shoulder as we boarded the plane stairs. I stepped to the side so my mom could get past.

"Yeah?" I winced, half expecting her to be mad at me for taking such a chance on her life with my bluff. I know I'd be upset if I were her. Mary joined her, threading her hand around my elbow.

"Good job out there," Grace said.

"Really? You'd have done the same thing?" I asked.

She snorted. "Not a chance. But maybe that's why we need you at the academy. We *all* think differently. And for the record—we knew about your father and what he did. Leo dug up your history the day you arrived. And yes, we still trusted you. Think we'd bring you all this way if we didn't? Give us some credit here, we're not dummies. You are *not* your father. It's obvious to anyone paying attention."

"Thanks," I said. "And I *am* sorry about risking your life like that. When I saw Mom, I snapped. The only reason I came to the academy was to keep her out of jail. When Zarn recruited me for the academy, he told me the government could punish her for allowing me to invent dangerous weapons. And like an idiot, I believed him. Seeing her all tied up like that—I can't even imagine . . ." I gulped at how bad things could have gotten.

"So, the only reason you agreed to come here was because some criminal lied about your mom being in danger?" Grace asked.

I bit my lip as I looked from her to Mary. That moment seemed so long ago. Since then, I'd discovered a new part of myself, one that had been hiding. And it had taken friendship to notice it. The team had let me be myself, and that was something I'd never found before. I'd been trying to control my relationships and keep people at bay, but that was like trying to harness lightning, when instead it's best to let it hit where it wants to and watch the show.

"You know what?" I blurted. "I'm glad he lied to me. Because I wouldn't have come to Genius Academy otherwise. And I never would have met any of you." The words were tumbling out now. "I'm sorry I didn't show you the note or my dad's keychain when I first saw them. I was scared you'd think I was in on Zarn's plan. I played right into his hands. I'm sorry I didn't trust you and even sorrier I didn't want to come to the academy in the first place." Relief flooded through me, but it was edged with fear. Being real with people made me nervous. I felt vulnerable without my shield.

"No worries, Tesla," Grace said, smacking me on the shoulder. "You're with us now. That's what matters." She ducked inside the plane to make sure Zarn was secured for our flight.

As usual, Mary read my mind. "You'll get used to it," she said airily, passing me to find a seat next to my mom.

I frowned at her. "Used to what?"

"Friends," she said simply. "Hi, Ms. Tesla. I'm Mary. Nikki's friend." She stuck her hand out to shake Mom's hand, as though they hadn't been through a near-death experience together minutes ago.

"Hello, Mary," Mom said, reaching in to give her a hug. "I don't know what they've been teaching you in that school of yours, but you really kept your head in that situation. Thank you for helping my daughter. Thank you *all*." She sniffed.

Mary beamed. "That's what friends are for, right?"

Mom gave me my third hug of the day. "I'm going to be having a long talk with whoever's in charge at that school of yours, young lady." Her voice was low. I stiffened. I would have some explaining to do when we got home. Would Mom pull me out of the academy after all? Tucking her face into my hair, she whispered, "But I'm proud of you."

Leo rushed toward the cockpit. "Shotgun!" he said. His cheeks turned red and he waggled his eyebrows. "Or should I say *death ray*?"

Grace groaned.

"What?" He shrugged. "Too soon?"

"Way too soon!" Charlie yelled, rolling her eyes.

"We'd better get moving, Nikki," Leo said, grabbing my hand and pulling me to the front of the plane. "I bet

Captain Pickles is annoyed at us for locking her in the cockpit, and she is not going to be able to fly this thing."

With Zarn deposited safely in the back of the plane and tied to a seat, we were ready to get home.

"Wait," Mom said, looking in the cockpit. "Where on earth is the pilot?!"

I bit my lip. "Um . . ." This would not go well. Saving the world from an evil genius was one thing, but flying a plane was another. I had a feeling her mind was about to be blown one more time. I was *so* grounded.

"You're looking at them, Ms. T," Leo said. He straightened up to greet her. "I'm Leo, by the way."

Mom's jaw dropped.

Leo gave her an easy smile. "I'm sorry, Ms. T, but there's no way to get one here anytime soon. We'd probably freeze to death first. You're going to have to trust us. I promise this is not the first time we've flown a jet."

I forced myself to keep a straight face. *But it is the second.*

"Come on, Mom," I whined. "You don't trust me?"

EPILOGUE

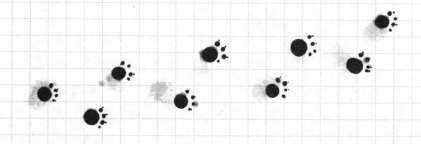

"Get out of my way, Pickles!" I threw a fry to the floor in an attempt to get my ferret off my latest invention. "We are *not* blowing a hole in the floor with this one. Do you hear me?"

Pickles skittered down to the shiny marble tile and began gnawing on her fry, holding it between her two paws like she was offering me a flower. She'd been living at the academy with me for three weeks now, ever since we got back from Ellesmere Island. Except for always sneaking into the kitchen, she was getting along pretty well. Charlie had even built her a special ferret fort to explore, next to my laboratory. (Did you catch that? I have a *real* laboratory now. So. Freaking. Cool.)

"Don't you realize how important this invention could be?" I asked her, grabbing a fry from the plate for myself. Along with incredible Rocky Road ice cream, Genius Academy also has a wonderful chef who makes the *best* fries. He even adds gravy just for Pickles, since he knows that's her favorite.

"Talking to yourself again, Nikki?" Leo stuck his head through the door. "Oh, hey, Pickles." He knelt down and stretched out his hand. Pickles hopped over to him, squirreling her way up his arm to sit on his shoulder. Watching Pickles play with Leo made my stomach twist up in a good way. The boy equation was still a mystery to me. Especially with Leo as a variable.

"You know it," I said. "What's up?"

He scratched under Pickles's chin and set her on my desk. "I have something for you," he said, tossing a plastic bag toward me.

"What's this?" I caught it, turning it over. It was small and light. I slid open the plastic seam and tipped the contents out into my palm. "New tech?"

Leo's eyes twinkled. "New *accessories*," he said.

I examined the tiny object. It was an atom pin, nearly identical to the one on my lapel. I narrowed my eyes, counting. My breath caught in my chest.

Instead of six electrons surrounding the nucleus, there were seven.

I slowly shook my head, my heart swelling with pride. "Seven electrons," I whispered. "Wow."

Nitrogen!!!

He stepped forward and took the pin from my hand. "Nitrogen," he said. He leaned close as he fixed it to my collar, brushing the flyaway strands of hair from the side of my neck. He smelled like mint toothpaste and his hair was still damp from the pool.

I stood still, unable to move.

Or *breathe*.

"We used to be carbon, of course. Six electrons," he continued. "But nitrogen is equally cool. It doesn't combine with other elements very well, *except* in the presence of a spark."

Those giant eagles were back. *A spark*.

He reached under my collar to remove the back from my old pin, his brow furrowed in concentration. "There," he said. He straightened the top of my shirt, grinning at his handiwork. "Now you're officially one of us."

"Thanks," I croaked, unable to stop the rush of heat from spreading through my face. He was still standing so close. And the side of my neck still buzzed from where he'd touched me.

Leo licked his lips, and his cheeks flushed pink. "I asked to be the one to give it to you. Starting today, that is our official academy pin. I wanted you to—"

"Yo!" A loud voice behind me made us both jump.

I spun around to face the door. Bert peeked in, a clip-board in his hand and a pencil stuck over his ear. He was out of breath.

"Am I interrupting something here?" he panted, his eyebrow quirked.

"Course not," I said, clearing my throat.

Just an incredibly amazing moment, you big giraffe. I avoided Bert's eyes and took a huge step back from Leo, shaking my head to clear it. The boy equation would have to be figured out another day.

"Situation Room in five," he said. "Martha just got off the phone with someone and it looks like we'll be taking another trip."

"Do you know where?" Leo asked.

Ever since we'd arrived home, Martha had been spending most of her time tracking down Zarn's associates, but so far she'd had little luck.

Bert gave us a conspiratorial look. "Well, she referred to the person on the other end of the line as '*Your Majesty*,' so my guess is some place with a monarchy."

I made a face. "That narrows it down."

Leaving the door of my lab open a crack so Pickles could roam the academy if she wanted, we hit the button for the elevator. After a beat, the doors slid open, revealing the rest of the team.

Charlie and Mary were practically vibrating. "I bet it was Prince Harry," Mary said. "Do you think it was Prince Harry?!" Bert rolled his eyes, and Grace hit the button for the top floor.

My stomach did its usual lurch as we approached Martha's massive office. The first time I visited her there, I'd thought I was about to get expelled. This time, a buzz of excitement started to sizzle through my body. Ever since Mom had agreed to let me stay at the academy (after a *very* long talk with Martha that I was not allowed to hear), even Martha didn't freak me out anymore.

At least, not as much as she *used* to.

She still has a bad habit of sneaking up on people though.

"Hi, Martha," we intoned as we entered her office. We sat in our respective chairs, still in their arched position around the front of her desk. An image of Buckingham Palace flickered on the screen to our right.

I nudged Mary, gesturing to the picture. Her eyes grew wide, and she poked Charlie to show her. *"Yes!"* She squirmed happily.

"Thank you for coming," Martha said. "I'm afraid there's been an incident, and it's of utmost importance that we attend to this matter straightaway. It's perhaps a sensitive topic, so I do apologize in advance for broaching the subject in this manner."

She was all business, even more than usual. Grace shifted in her chair nervously. "What is it, Martha? How can we help?"

She leveled her gaze at me. "Nikki, your father is alive."

To Be Continued

AUTHOR'S NOTE

All the characters and events in this book are fiction, yet they are based on some real-life people who have had incredible adventures in human history. You may know some of their names already. (Perhaps you've even seen some of their famous creations, like Leonardo da Vinci's *Mona Lisa*.)

To learn more about the real-life people who inspired the characters in this book, I highly recommend you speak to your librarian or teacher. I had a great time reimagining them as children working together at Genius Academy, but their true genius and accomplishments will always be cooler than any fiction. Enjoy exploring their histories!

Nikola Tesla (inventor)

Grace O'Malley (Irish pirate queen)

Leonardo da Vinci (polymath and artist)

Wolfgang Amadeus Mozart (musical prodigy)

Albert Einstein (physicist and visionary)

Charles Darwin (biologist)

Mary Shelley (author)

ABOUT NIKOLA TESLA

In the book, the character of Nikki Tesla is a reimagined version of Nikola Tesla, an accomplished (male!) Serbian inventor born in 1856. Tesla was also an engineer, physicist, and futurist, with a mind so brilliant, the rest of the world often struggled to keep up. You know that smartphone that you use to chat with your friends? Tesla predicted smartphone technology in 1926. He also invented the alternating current generator that is used to light up your house this very day. Nikola Tesla also developed the concepts and technology for radio, X-rays, wireless communications, modern electric motors, and even invented the remote control. He was also famous for his generosity, sharing his ideas and patents with others. Oh, and he could speak eight languages, and recite entire books he'd memorized at will.

You might be wondering: Did Tesla invent a death ray?

Some believe he did.

The "teleforce" was an invention said to send concentrated beams of particles through the air with such tremendous energy that it would bring down 10,000 airplanes at a distance of 250 miles. Tesla hoped that his invention could be used to help put a stop to wars. Today, many experts believe the idea to be unrealistic. But if there's one thing I've learned about Tesla, it's that he should never be underestimated.

ACKNOWLEDGMENTS

This book is filled with reimagined geniuses, and I am lucky to be surrounded by many real-life geniuses who helped me bring it to life. I wish I could give everyone a celebratory pet ferret!

Thank you to Abby McAden for welcoming me to the Scholastic family, and to Jenne Abramowitz for your amazing editorial eye, incredible comedic timing, and guidance on this series. To Keirsten Geise, Josh Berlowitz, and Shelly Romero: Thank you all so much for making this book not only fun and easy to read but also beautiful, as well! To Lissy Marlin, illustrator extraordinaire, thank you for bringing your magic to every page!

To Tracy van Straaten, Rachel Feld, Lizette Serrano, Anne Marie Wong, Anne Shone, Diane Kerner, Jenn Hubbs, and Denise Anderson: You are all such joys to work with—thank you so much for all you do to get this book into the hands of readers. I'm so fortunate to be on your team!

To Justin, my family, and friends: Thank you all for the love, support, and brainstorming sessions. And of course, no acknowledgments would be complete without Kathleen Rushall, my brilliant agent and friend. You are a poetic and noble land mermaid, Kat. This journey just wouldn't be right without you.

Finally, thank you to the children's lit community, the Nerdy Book Club, and every librarian, educator, bookseller, and parent out there working hard to foster curiosity and passion in your kids. You're saving the world. I hope this book sparks something wonderful, wherever you are.

AUTHOR BIO

Jess Keating has been sprayed by skunks, bitten by crocodiles, and victim of the dreaded paper cut. Her books blend science, humor, and creativity, and include the acclaimed My Life Is a Zoo middle-grade trilogy and award-winning picture books, like *Shark Lady* and *Pink Is for Blobfish*. Jess lives in Ontario, Canada, where she loves hiking, nerdy documentaries, and writing books for adventurous and funny kids. Jess can be found online at jesskeating.com or on Twitter at @Jess_Keating.